She was a professional. On duty.

She didn't have time to picture running her fingers through that messy hair of his. Or...or... Her gaze rose from his mouth, quirking up at the corners as it was, to meet his eyes. They really were the soft blue of a star sapphire. She curled her fingers against her belt. Would the stubble on his face be rough or as soft as his hair looked?

"Darlin', you really shouldn't look at a man that way." His gruff voice was both a caress and a wake-up call.

Quin barely controlled a full-body shudder. She needed to think of ice baths and blizzards. Snow and ski slopes. High mountain air. Invigorating. Not warm. Not sexy. She took that step back, both physically and mentally. He laughed and the sound was dark and warm like fudge brownies just out of the oven. Her mouth watered.

Coffee. She needed coffee. And fresh air. Like right this minute.

Dear Reader,

Thirty-five years ago, I was asked to do a novel for a new line: Silhouette Desire. It was quite an honor, as I'd only been a published author for three years. So I said yes, and the novel I produced was *The Cowboy and the Lady*, which came out in 1982. At that time, I was a full-time newspaper reporter and the mother of a two-year-old son.

I loved Desire from the day they bought that first book. The Desire line, now Harlequin Desire, was racy and passionate, and we were allowed a lot of freedom within the confines of traditional category romance.

It has been my pleasure to write for that wonderful line many times over the past thirty-five years. I've enjoyed every story I got to tell. But *The Cowboy and the Lady* is still my favorite, of all the books I've ever written. Jason Whitehall was a unique character, much easier to dislike than like as the story began. And Amanda, my heroine, was innocent. I can't tell you how many editors I had to fight at other houses to maintain my virginal heroines. But I never had to fight a Harlequin editor to create heroines who reflected my own set of values. Harlequin Desire always made me feel at home and welcome.

I will always treasure my Desire novels. They hold a special place in my heart, as does the Harlequin Desire line. Happy 35th Anniversary!

Diana Palmer

SILVER JAMES

—

THE COWBOY'S
CHRISTMAS PROPOSITION

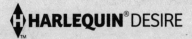

As always, thanks to my family for putting up with the craziness when I'm on deadline—and that includes my wonderful Harlequin Desire team, Charles, Stacy and Tahra, plus all the amazing Harlequin folks. And a special thanks to a special reader, Anita Bartlett, for our discussion of brothers from a sister's point of view.

ISBN-13: 978-0-373-83876-9

The Cowboy's Christmas Proposition

Copyright © 2017 by Silver James

Recycling programs for this product may not exist in your area.

HARLEQUIN® www.Harlequin.com

Printed in U.S.A.

Silver James likes walks on the wild side and coffee. Okay. She LOVES coffee. A cowgirl at heart, she's been an army officer's wife and mom, and worked in the legal field, fire service and law enforcement. Now retired from the real world, she lives in Oklahoma, spending her days writing with the assistance of two Newfoundlands, the cat who rules them all and the characters living in her imagination.

Books by Silver James

Harlequin Desire

Red Dirt Royalty

Cowgirls Don't Cry
The Cowgirl's Little Secret
The Boss and His Cowgirl
Convenient Cowgirl Bride
Redeemed by the Cowgirl
Claiming the Cowgirl's Baby
The Cowboy's Christmas Proposition

Visit her Author Profile page at Harlequin.com, or silverjames.com, for more titles.

Dear Reader,

With this book, the Red Dirt Royalty series shifts from the Barron brothers to their Tate cousins. Fitting, since the series is about families, about the good times and the bad, and about making new families. Of the seven Tate brothers, it was Deacon who "stepped to the microphone"—unsurprising given his career as a country singing star—to tell me his story first.

Family is important to Deacon. Celebrations and anniversaries are all icing on his cake and he's always happy to support his family with a special song or an unexpected appearance. Oklahoma Highway Patrol trooper Quincy Kincaid, on the other hand, has a jaded view of families and holidays. Watching her discover what love is all about was a fun trip. I hope you'll enjoy coming along for the ride.

Everyone needs romance in their lives and Harlequin Desire has been delivering happily-ever-afters for thirty-five years. October marks Desire's 35th anniversary. Join with me and all the Harlequin Desire authors to celebrate! There is virtual cake and champagne and lots of handsome heroes and feisty heroines, including Deacon and Quin.

Here's a toast to Harlequin Desire and to you, faithful reader, to celebrate romance:

To love is nothing, to be loved is something, to love and be loved is everything.

Here's to happy reading...and everything! Cheers!

Silver James

One

Deacon Tate was a country boy at heart. He loved life on his Oklahoma ranch—driving the tractor, singing to the cows, riding his horse and stopping to watch the setting sun wash a blaze of colors across the red dirt of home. He would sit on his front porch as twilight softened the landscape, strumming his guitar while waiting for the fireflies to come out to play. He was also a free spirit. He loved life on the road, living on the tour bus, appearing in a different city every night. He fed off the energy of the crowd, absorbing their excitement through his skin by osmosis.

Performing live was in his blood, but he was ready for some downtime in his Red, White and Cool tour. The Sons of Nashville's manager had purposely scheduled this leg of the tour close to home. After tonight's performance at the Thunder River Casino just outside of Oklahoma City, the band would take off the week before Thanksgiving and Deke would be heading home to his ranch. Then the Friday after, they had a concert at the BOK Center in Tulsa. They were done for a month after that. The break couldn't come soon enough.

He sang into the microphone, but his eyes were on the female fans lining the front of the stage trying to get his attention. He flirted with them with winks, and by appearing to sing directly to one or another. He loved women. All women. And he'd only been exclusive once.

The lights dimmed, a stool appeared on stage and he picked up his acoustic guitar and sat down. One blue spotlight picked him out. Head down, he strummed a few chords. The cheers and whistles slowly faded as he played. The chords gave way to the melody he plucked on the strings. The band remained silent, unsure of where he was going. Performing this song was totally unplanned. He'd written it for his cousin Cash's wedding but hadn't recorded it.

Deke's little brother, who was also the keyboardist for the Sons, was the first to recognize the song. After Dillon's piano riff, their guitarists, Bryce and Xander, picked up the tune and Kenji, the drummer, found the rhythm. Ozzie picked up the bass line without missing a beat.

"Are you ready to take a walk?" he crooned into the microphone. "Darlin', are you ready for me?" The crowd started to sway in time to the music and the groupies lining the stage pressed forward. Deke closed his eyes. "Are you counting the minutes? Can you feel my heart race?" He riffed on the guitar. "From this day forward, you'll never walk alone. I'll shelter your heart. I'll be your home. You are my love song, my forever song, the last song that I'll sing."

He poured out the rest of the words, his voice growing husky with emotion. Deke had watched each of his cousins find and fall in love with the women who completed them. Something inside him wanted the same thing, in a vague someday way. But none of his brothers had taken the plunge and there was something wrong with that picture. The Barrons were the wild bunch, the Tates the steady gatekeepers. Well, except for him. His mother said often and loudly that he was more Barron than Tate, but her eyes twinkled when she said it.

Deke sang of finding love, of losing it. He sang of getting it back and when he sang the chorus again, the women in the front row had faces slick with tears. His voice broke a little as he finished the last few lines and added, "You'll be my home, my love song, my forever song and the last song I ever sing."

The spotlight went out. Stunned silence filled the theater, where 2,500 fans were jammed in wall-to-wall. Then pandemonium erupted. Strobes flashed and spotlights probed the stage, but Deacon had disappeared. People screamed and whistled. They clapped their hands and stomped their feet. When the band launched into the opening strains of "Native Son," the noise volume doubled. Normally, this song was the finale but tonight, it was the encore.

When it was over, Deke and the band retreated backstage to the dressing rooms. The party had already started. Local radio personalities filtered in, some with contest winners tagging along. A few VIPs—politicians and business leaders—crowded around, congratulating him before moving along to the free bar and buffet. A low-level headache throbbed behind his eyes, and Deke only wanted to get on his bus and go home.

A loud squeal caught his attention and he looked up just in time to catch an armful of curves and red hair. Lips smacked his cheek. "You sang our song!" Roxanne Barron screamed.

Deke winced and was thankful when his cousin Cash peeled his wife away. He was surrounded now by family. His brothers, Cooper and Bridger, were harassing Dillon, the baby Tate. Cash was doing his best to contain Roxie, while his other cousins and their spouses, Chance and Cassidy, along with Cord and Jolie, laughed.

"You totally have to record that song, Deke," Cassidy said. "And have Jolie and I mentioned that we're totally PO'd you didn't write songs for our weddings?"

He ducked his head, slightly embarrassed. He'd been on the road and missed both Chance's and Cord's weddings though he'd played a cover song at their brother Clay's. Forcing his headache away, he listened to his cousins and their wives chatter and his brothers tease Dillon. This was family and he loved his.

There was life and love here. Sound and confusion. Friendship and flirting. Deke wasn't quite so ready to go home now, knowing his house was empty. There'd be no lights on, unless someone had gone by. He had a ranch foreman who lived on the property, keeping an eye on things when Deke was on the road or recording in Nashville, but he doubted the man would think of switching on lights.

The party finally wrapped up and those who lingered spilled into the parking lot. The band would ride the tour bus to Oklahoma City. Those who lived in Nashville had reservations at the Barron Hotel. They'd sleep during what was left of the night and fly home later in the day.

The roadies would break down the sets, instruments and sound systems, and leave the semitrucks and trailers in the secured storage yard where the local guys stored their vehicles during tours. That was where Deacon had left his pickup. He was ready to get home, even if the place would be dark and silent when he arrived.

"Mr. Tate!" The agitated yell disrupted his reverie; he and his three brothers all looked up. "Deacon!" The tour bus driver, Max, clarified. He was all but jumping up and down, alternating between waving and wringing his hands.

"Maxie? What's going on?"

"I didn't know what to do, Mr. T. I called the police and I was gettin' ready to come inside to get you but I couldn't leave it."

"Calm down, Max. Police? Why would you—" Deke's question was interrupted by a loud wail.

The driver pointed at a basket perched on the curving steps leading into the bus. "That's why, Mr. T. I found a baby."

* * *

Quincy Kincaid carefully sipped the hot coffee in her to-go cup. Five more hours until her shift change at 7:00 a.m. Her night had been quiet so far. A few speeders. Backing up a Cleveland County deputy on a domestic. She checked the dash clock on her Highway Patrol cruiser. Four hours, fifty-five minutes. And then she was off for three days before her next set of duty days, putting her that much closer to her vacation. Seventeen days, most of them spent far away from everyone. And one more item marked off her bucket list.

Aspen, Colorado, and Rocky Mountain high country, here she came. She'd saved up vacation time and money for this trip since she'd graduated from the Oklahoma Highway Patrol academy five years before. Five-star hotel. Beautiful scenery. Learning to ski. And Christmas far away from her family. She wasn't a Scrooge. Christmas was okay. It was her family that drove her batty.

Another sip of coffee, and she discovered it was cool enough to drink without caution but still hot enough to be satisfying. Thunder River Truck Stop always had fresh coffee, no matter the time of day or night. She gazed toward the bright splash of LED lights just over a mile down the road. The casino, like the truck stop, was a 24-7-365 operation. She'd set up here earlier and had caught some speeders leaving the concert. Deacon Tate and the Sons of Nashville. The concert had sold out and she'd been lucky not to get roped into extra security duty at the casino. That had gone to the off-duty guys who wanted to pick up extra money for Christmas.

The only present she was buying this Christmas was for herself—the trip to Aspen, to stay in that five-star hotel through the holidays. No family—not that hers really cared. No responsibilities and woo-hoo for that. Just snow and pine trees and mountains and, if she was lucky, a hot guy to share drinks with while sitting in front of a roaring fire. Quin rolled her head on her neck and eased the tightness in her shoulders. Only four hours and forty—

"Adam-109." The dispatcher's voice crackled from her radio.

"Adam-109."

"Respond to Thunder River Casino. In the parking lot. Report of a found infant."

She opened her mouth to respond when the import of the message filtered through her brain. "Say again, Dispatch."

"Report of a found infant, Adam-109. Look for the Sons of Nashville tour bus."

"Ten-four."

Seriously? A found baby? Who loses their baby? *Oh, wait*, she thought sarcastically. She was headed to a casino. People addicted to gambling did dumb things. Like losing their kids. Still, what did the band's bus have to do with the situation? Good thing she was less than five minutes away. She'd be able to satisfy her curiosity quickly. Unable to resist, she hit her overhead emergency lights but without sirens. Traffic stopped on the highway to let her exit the truck stop and she gunned her engine.

The tour bus wasn't hard to miss. It was one of those custom motor coaches that cost more than most people's houses. Why people would call such a lavish vehicle a bus was beyond her comprehension. She'd worked event security a few times. Spoiled musicians and Hollywood people just irritated her.

She rolled up on the scene and notified Dispatch. Settling her Smokey Bear hat on her head, she stepped out of her cruiser, adjusted her weapons belt on her hips and strode toward the knot of people gathered around the open door of the motor coach.

A dark-haired woman was arguing with a tall man dressed like a cowboy holding a bundle in his arms. As Quin walked up, she overheard him say, "Forget it, Jolie. You can't have her."

Quin sighed. Was she walking into another domestic, only without backup this time?

"I just want to hold her," the woman pleaded. "You let Cassie hold her. Besides, I'm a nurse. I should check her, make sure she's okay." The woman peered down at the bundle and cooed.

Someone dramatically cleared his throat and the entire group turned to look at Quin. She inhaled, set a stern expression on her face and trudged toward them. "I'm Trooper Kincaid," she announced. "What's going on here?"

Everyone started talking at once. Quin's piercing whistle silenced them—all except the baby, who was now crying. The guy holding the infant shifted positions, patting its back as he sort of did this dip-and-sway thing with the kid on his shoulder. The wails turned to little sobs and after a hiccup, the baby cooed, settling its head against the cowboy's chest.

"I'm Deacon Tate," the cowboy explained.

Of course he was. Quin would have banged her head against the side of the bus if she'd been standing close enough. "Is that your baby, Mr. Tate?"

"Not exactly."

"Care to explain?"

"Someone left her on my bus."

"There was a note," a beautiful blonde added helpfully.

"And Max found her," a redhead explained.

An older man wearing a plaid flannel shirt covering a paunch that hung over his belt buckle offered a little wave. "I drive the bus," he explained.

Quin closed her eyes. She hadn't had enough caffeine to deal with groupies and good-ol'-boy bus drivers, much less stars too handsome for her taste. When she opened her eyes, no one had moved. She pointed at the driver as she pulled out a notebook and pen. "You. Tell me your full name and what happened?"

"Max, ma'am. Max Padilla. After the concerts, I hang around backstage until the after-party starts to break up. Then I come out and warm up the bus. It's a diesel so it runs rough on cold nights if I don't. Plus, I like to get the heat goin' in the back so the guys are warm, you know?"

Holding on to her patience, Quin prompted, "The baby?"

"Well, yeah. I was gettin' to that. So anyway, I came out to start the bus and there was the usual stuff stacked up around the door."

"The usual stuff?"

"Yeah. Flowers and…" The man stared at his boots. Was he blushing? "And stuff that girls—fans—leave for Deacon and the boys."

"Stuff. What kind of stuff?"

A guy who looked Asian leaned forward. "We get love notes and T-shirts and—"

"Bras and panties," a younger version of Deacon Tate explained.

Why her? She was so close to end of shift. Quin made a pointed notation in her book: *Stuff!* She looked up, pretending Deacon didn't steal her breath. "And?"

When Deacon's younger clone opened his mouth, Deacon himself cut him off. "Shut up, Dillon. There was a basket tucked in with all the stuff." He glanced through the bus doors, and Quin noticed a wicker basket for the first time. "Little Noelle here was inside all bundled up in blankets with her diaper bag."

"You know her name?"

Another man, just as handsome as Deacon but with darker hair and eyes—because she'd just realized Deacon's were blue—stepped closer, an envelope in his hand, and introduced himself. "I'm Chance Barron."

That was a name she was familiar with. The Barron family attorney. Just jolly. Her night kept getting better and better. "And you are here why, Mr. Barron?"

"Deacon is my cousin. My wife, Cassie, and I were here for the concert."

"I'm Jolie Barron," the brunette added. "I'm an RN and I can check her over if my big goof of a cousin-in-law will give me a chance to hold her."

So these were *not* groupies. Quin studied everyone in the group of people standing around. Tates and Barrons were easy to categorize. That left the motley crew likely making up Deacon's band the Sons of Nashville. *Yippee.* She wondered if she could call this in and let Cleveland County handle it. As she mulled over that idea, another police vehicle rolled to a stop next to her cruiser. Chickasaw Tribal Police. The casino and surrounding area were technically tribal land. Maybe she'd just let them have it.

"The note that came in the basket states the child's name is Noelle and that she belongs to Deacon," Chance continued as the tribal cops approached.

She took the proffered piece of paper and read it before handing it to the nearest tribal officer. Quin arched a brow at the country music superstar. "How often does your…" She didn't want to say "baby momma." Considering who she was dealing with, she had to proceed cautiously. "Has this happened before? Your child being dropped off like this?"

"No." Deacon's voice was one step above a growl. The baby fussed and he automatically soothed her. "I'm not irresponsible, Trooper Kincaid. I don't have any children." He paused, then added, "That I know of."

Quin glanced at the Chickasaw officers and one shrugged. "Unless she's Indian, we don't have jurisdiction. You're state. Up to you to place her with DHS."

The Department of Human Services—the foster

care system. Quin knew what that was like. She'd been in the system as a kid. She was reluctant to sentence a baby to Child Protective Services but she didn't have much choice. She keyed the portable radio mic clipped to her shoulder. "Adam-109, Dispatch. Notify DHS of an emergency pickup notice for an infant, my location."

Dispatch's response was drowned out by loud objections from the Tates and Barrons. One voice rose above all the rest.

"DHS can't have her. According to the note, she's mine."

Two

What the heck was he thinking? Deke *knew* this baby wasn't his. Or was she? He took precautions, though there was always a chance something might go wrong. Without knowing who the baby's mother was, he wouldn't be able to say for sure one way or the other. If he had any sense at all, he would hand her off to the female trooper—and why had he never noticed how sexy a woman in uniform could be? This one nipped at him like one of those yappy little ankle-biter dogs. He glanced at her, assessing the expression on her face. Okay, make that a Doberman.

Noelle cooed and rubbed her cheek against his shoulder. He always had been a sucker for little kids and the idea of this one going to strangers… He halted that thought because, okay, *he* was a stranger. But he wasn't. Her mother had claimed he was the father and left the baby's basket outside his bus for a reason.

Fatherhood. The idea was like that charity ice-bucket challenge—chilling but with warm fuzzies underneath for doing something good.

Hadn't he spent the last hour contemplating family then going home to an empty house? A baby would complicate things but if Noelle *was* his, he'd step up and take care of her. Katherine Tate hadn't raised her boys to shuck their responsibilities. He might be full-grown but his mom would take a strip out of his hide if he didn't do the right thing.

Noelle cooed and his heart did a funny little lurch in his chest. The idea of being her father didn't seem quite so alien now. He tested the word *dad* in his head. It didn't freak him out—and it probably should have.

He glanced toward Chance, who shifted position so the trooper couldn't see Deke. His cousin mouthed the words, *Are you sure you want the baby?* Deke stared into Chance's eyes and nodded. Chance moved away from the group, phone pressed to his ear. Man, but it was nice to have a hotshot attorney right there. Things settled in his chest and he liked the feeling. He'd always wanted to be a dad, but at some nebulous point in the future. Maybe this was fate's way of telling him the time was now. Taking on the care and feeding of baby Noelle was the right thing to do. Yeah, this was the right thing for him to do.

"Have you thought this through, Mr. Tate?" The cop was still glaring at him through narrowed eyes.

"I have, Trooper Kincaid." He offered her the smile

where his dimple peeked out. "Do you have a first name?"

"Yes. How are you going to take care of her?"

"What is it?" He'd like to take care of the trooper, for sure. The more he studied her, from her brown felt Smokey Bear hat to her shiny black roper boots, the more he felt that way.

"Are you avoiding my question, Mr. Tate?"

"No. What's your name?"

"Persistent, aren't you?"

"I am when I'm after something I want."

She blinked a few times as she tucked her chin in and leaned away. He'd surprised her. Her light-colored eyes narrowed and her generous mouth thinned out as she pressed her lips together in a disapproving sneer.

"I told you my name. It's Trooper Kincaid."

"I'm Deacon, Troop, but my friends call me Deke."

"I'm not your friend, Mr. Tate."

"But you could be."

She glanced around as if suddenly realizing they had an audience. He liked that he'd put her off balance. She hit him with a steely-eyed, no-nonsense glare. Deke was enjoying teasing her far too much.

"Mr. Tate. Please hand over—" Noelle wailed and the trooper looked panicked.

Deke patted the baby's bottom. Yup. The kid was wet. "I do believe she needs a diaper change." He turned for the bus.

Jolie stepped forward wearing what he called her stern-mother face. "I'll take the baby inside to change her."

As a guy, Deke should have turned over the task automatically, but he suddenly found himself oddly protective and...possessive of the baby. "I'm perfectly capable of changing a wet diaper, Jolie. Not the first time I've done it." He glanced at Cash and Dillon. "You two certainly gave me enough practice when I got stuck with babysitting duty."

Before Jolie—or anyone else—could argue, Deke snagged the basket, which still held the diaper bag, and climbed the curving stairs into the main living space of the coach. There were two captain chairs—one for the driver, the other for a copilot—just beyond the door.

Inside, leather couches the color of pewter flanked an eating area with a table and two benches next to the kitchenette. The walls were tiger-eye maple. The counters and tables were topped in granite veined with a handful of colors ranging from black to rusty pink to white. Deke dropped the basket and bag on the couch next to the table.

He heard someone clomping up the steps behind him. Without turning around, he knew who had followed him. "Have a seat, Troop. I'll be right back." He paused before heading to the back of the bus, again giving her the once-over. Her tan slacks were tailored to fit and not even the bulletproof vest beneath the dark brown uniform shirt could contain her curves. She'd slicked back her hair under the Smokey Bear hat and he couldn't tell the color, but thought it was blond or light brown. He really wanted to see the color of her eyes but the hat brim kept them shaded.

Trooper Kincaid wasn't the type of woman who

usually caught his attention. Groupies knew the rules, played the game. Maybe he was intrigued because she was something different. Her stern authority didn't fit in his world, but there was some undefined *something* that drew him. He'd have to think about why later. First things first.

"Dig around in the bag for wipes, a fresh diaper and something to change her into, will ya? This onesie is wet now."

"This onesie is wet now?" Quin muttered as she bent over the couch and opened the diaper bag. "How does the man even know what a onesie is?" By the time he got back with several towels to pad the table, she'd found the items he requested. She noticed the wet spot on his chest. That explained the need for a clothing change but she was still mystified as to how he knew what the garment was called. She watched as he got to work, fascinated despite her best intentions.

This guy had *bad boy* written all over him. Now that she could see him in decent lighting, his sheer male magnetism hit her like a tackle from a Dallas Cowboys linebacker. He was undeniably handsome, with thick brown hair that fell around his high cheekbones and sculpted jaw. Five-o'clock shadow added a rugged layer to his face. Wide-set blue eyes held a twinkle that reminded her of a star-sapphire ring she once had. His black Western shirt and leather jeans fit him far too thoroughly for the welfare of the general female population. Herself included.

His fingers were long and dexterous, as would befit

a guitarist, and he deftly changed the baby's diaper and clothing. He wore a leather thong around his neck and Noelle snagged it in one chubby hand. Deacon laughed and cooed at her, like he did this all the time. For all Quin knew, he might.

She tried to sift a bio for him out of her crowded brain. Not that she was a big watcher of entertainment gossip shows. Still, Barrons and Tates were often covered in the local news, but she couldn't recall hearing that he was married—or ever had been.

"Did you find any bottles in the bag? Or a can of formula or something?"

Lost in her musings, she startled at the sound of his voice. Luckily, he was still concentrating on the baby so he hadn't noticed she'd been staring at his butt this whole time. "Oh, yes. There are a couple of full bottles. Not sure what's in them."

He glanced her way, and that killer smile with a side of dimple guaranteed to dampen groupies' panties appeared. Quin refused to let it work on her. Much. She curled her fingers against her palms because they itched to push his hair back off his face and then tangle in the thick waves. His gaze focused on her mouth and she couldn't stop her quick inhalation, nor could she keep her chest from swelling and pushing against the rigid bulk of her bulletproof vest. This man was lethal and she needed to remember that.

He held out his hand and she passed one of the bottles to him. Deacon twisted off the lid, sniffed and then dipped his finger in to taste, which was such a guy thing to do. "Formula. I think. Let's pop it in the microwave for about fifteen seconds. We don't want it too hot." He caught her gaze on him, and the stars in his sapphire eyes blazed. "The formula, that is."

Quin just managed to avoid rolling her eyes. She wasn't some teenage fangirl fawning over the magnificent Deacon Tate. She retrieved the bottle from him and dumped it in the sink. "I'll make fresh." She snagged a can with a baby on the label and read the instructions. She pretended the whole time that her fingers hadn't tingled when they touched his skin. That her nose hadn't gotten a whiff of clean sweat and a scent deeper and more primal when she handed the bottle back to him. He settled on the couch.

Opting for discretion over valor because her body was fomenting mutiny, she retreated across the bus and sat on the matching couch to watch. She still couldn't get over how proficiently this guy handled the baby.

"You said you don't have kids?" she finally asked, removing her hat.

His gaze was sharp as he looked up. "Kinda hard to have kids without a wife."

That didn't stop a lot of celebrities but she didn't point that out. "Then how are you so good with the baby?"

He paused to burp the infant then cuddled her back in one arm with the bottle in her mouth. Quin attempted to read the expression on Deacon's face. She found a sweetness there that was almost as surprising as his competence.

"Only child?"

"Excuse me?"

"Not a hard question, Troop."

"Stop calling me that."

"Then tell me your first name."

Quin refused to throw her hands up in a fit of frustration. "Fine. Not that it's any of your business, but it's Quincy."

"Did you hear that, Noelle? Her name is Quincy."

The baby cooed, and Quin discovered she was grinning rather stupidly. She wiped that expression off her face and leaned forward so she could breathe a little easier in her vest. "And to answer your question, I'm not an only child. I have four older brothers."

Deacon peeked up at her from under lashes far too long and lush for a man exuding as much testosterone as this one did. "Ah, the baby in the family. I'm the middle and got stuck with baby duty, especially with Dillon. He was a late surprise for Mom and Dad."

She glanced out the tinted window behind her. "Dillon is in your band?"

"Yup."

"Was he serious?"

"About what?"

"The...*stuff*?" She wanted to bite her tongue. She didn't care if overenthusiastic fans embarrassed themselves by leaving underwear in tribute to the band. Nor did she care if maybe some of the owners of said lingerie ended up in the bedroom or one of the curtained bunks she could see when she glanced toward the back of the bus.

He laughed and set the bottle on the table. Shifting the baby to his shoulder, he patted her back until she burped again. Deacon checked her diaper, settled her back in the crook of his arm and gazed at Quin. "Yeah, he was serious. We get stuff like that thrown on stage sometimes, too. Goes with the gig."

She couldn't decide if he was being this nonchalant because he was so egotistical that he figured the thongs and *stuff* were his due or because he didn't care. Time was passing and Quin needed to get things wrapped up. "Is she really yours?"

"Who?"

"The baby," she said pointedly.

He studied her face and she flushed for no reason she understood. He broke their staring match first by peering down at the sleeping infant. That soft expression washed over his features again, and she wondered where the feelings came from. Maybe Noelle really was his. Her chest burned at the thought, and she didn't quite know how to handle the feeling. To cover it up, she asked again, "Is the baby yours, Mr. Tate?"

Before he answered her question, the sound of booted feet stomping up the steps drew their attention to the front of the bus. Chance Barron's gaze bounced between her and Deacon before he announced, "She is until you find her mother, Trooper Kincaid, and we clear things up."

Three

Deke didn't know whether to high-five his cousin or panic. Was his ego overriding his common sense on the outside chance Noelle was his? Babies were hard. He knew that, but while he didn't quite understand his attraction to the gruff cop, he was adamant about keeping the baby close until he knew definitively who the father was. Noelle was a cute little thing and deserved something more than becoming a ward of the state.

So yeah, he'd score this one for the good guys. Not that Quincy Kincaid was a bad guy. She wasn't a *guy* in any way, shape or form. She'd pushed to her feet when Chance came in. With her back to Deke, he could tell the hair twisted into a tight knot at the base of her neck was blond.

His blood warmed. There was something about the

nape of a woman's neck that really stirred him up.
Some men liked breasts, some a sweetly rounded butt.
Him? The arch of a woman's neck and the lines of her
back. He loved kissing his way down from the spot
where a woman's hair met skin on her nape, across
soft shoulders and down the valley of her spine. Shifting uncomfortably, he jerked his thoughts away from
Quincy the woman to focus on Quincy the cop.

"I don't think you understand the situation, Mr. Barron. A Child Protection worker from DHS will be here
shortly. Under the law, Mr. Tate has to relinquish custody. He has no proof the child is his."

"You're the one who doesn't understand, Trooper
Kincaid." Chance stepped toward her, his phone held
out. "I'll have the paper version of this court order here
very likely before your DHS representative arrives."

Deacon exchanged a relieved look with his cousin
while Quincy scanned the document on Chance's
phone.

"Who can call a judge at three thirty in the morning
and get a custody order signed?" she muttered. Inhaling in an obvious—to him anyway—effort to control
her frustration, she passed the phone back to Chance.
She added, more loudly, "We'll all just sit right here
until DHS and your paperwork arrive. In the meantime, Mr. Tate—"

"Deke," he insisted.

"Mr. Tate." She arched one brow and glowered. "In
the meantime, you can explain to me how you, a single
man, plan to care for a baby girl. I seriously doubt this
bus contains a nursery."

"Considering I'm headed home as soon as we settle things, it doesn't matter if it does or not."

He watched her pull in her chin, crinkle her forehead and scowl at him. Deke was just contrary enough to enjoy the heck out of putting that expression on her face.

"So, you have a nursery set up at your home? Which is where, by the way? You can't take the baby back to Nashville."

"Home is a ranch about an hour's drive from here. And I admit I don't exactly have a nursery."

"Yet," Chance interjected. "Cassie, Jolie and Roxie have gone shopping. You will have everything you need by the time we get this worked out."

"Wait until Mom hears about this." Deke all but chortled. His mother was huge on family and none of her wayward sons had provided her with a grandchild. None of them was married. As a result, she doted on Cord and Jolie's little boy, CJ.

Quin favored Chance and him with her scowl. She'd been outfoxed and her expression indicated she knew it. She stepped back as Chance approached him but he could see the wheels turning. She hadn't surrendered. Yet. And wouldn't it be sweet when she did.

Chance murmured in his ear, "Won't be anything fancy. They went to the all-night supercenter." He glanced down at the baby and got a goofy look on his face. Deke choked back a laugh. If Noelle stayed in the family for very long, he predicted a Barron baby boom by next autumn.

Pulling back mentally, Deke considered what he'd just thought. He wasn't as freaked out by the notion of keeping Noelle in the family as he probably should be. That idea was all sorts of wrong. He toured. A lot. Only coming home when he could. He could hire a nanny, keep Noelle on the road with him. Or leave her at home with a nanny… Nope. He didn't like that idea at all. He did like the idea of having a loving wife and family—no matter where he was. Only that idea was all sorts of wrong, too.

Wow. He knew that the magic baby smell worked on testosterone as easily as it did on estrogen, but it was supposed to have the opposite effect. Women were supposed to go all weird and want babies. Not men. So why was he going all mushy where the kid was concerned? Deke was honest enough to admit his head space had been strange all night long. And then he was hit with the possibility that he had a kid. He'd been blindsided, but he'd also responded viscerally to the idea. It was growing on him.

He barely noticed Chance leave as he stared down at the baby in his arms. The little imp had obviously bewitched him. He'd never lacked for female companionship, and until his rather maudlin reflections of earlier, being tied down with a wife and family was a foreign concept. Maybe his cousins' happiness *was* rubbing off on him. Maybe he just needed something more than a one-night stand. Maybe he'd get lucky with the very luscious Trooper Quincy Kincaid. Maybe she'd even wear her Smokey Bear hat.

Noelle whimpered in her sleep, reminding him of what was at stake here. Deep down, he knew that as soon as the baby's mother was located—and his family had the resources to find her—the situation would be straightened out. When it was, he'd get back to life as normal—a life full of long-legged cowgirls in Daisy Dukes while touring, then going home and sitting on his front porch with a cold beer and his guitar for company.

Quin's voice interrupted his reverie. "I don't believe for a minute you are naive enough to believe that baby is yours."

With one hand, he grabbed the basket and moved it closer. With profound gentleness, he transferred the little girl into it. She stayed asleep. After tucking a crocheted blanket around her, he brushed the tip of his index finger through her wispy gold baby hair.

The sexy cop standing a few feet away kept pinging his radar. She'd been gruff and in-your-face about Noelle, and he wanted to know what made her tick. They had some time to kill. He'd watched out the window as his brothers and Cash Barron organized rides and shipped almost everyone off.

Deke wanted to satisfy his curiosity about Trooper Kincaid and whether she was as aloof—and as immune to him—as she pretended to be. He watched her from under half-lidded eyes, not missing a detail. Shoulders back, feet apart, knees slightly bent, hand on the butt of her pistol. She looked like she was getting ready for a fight.

"Do I make you nervous?" he drawled.

Quin refused to retreat a step, though her common sense insisted it was the smart thing to do. Instead, she stood her ground. She was the trained law-enforcement officer here. She was in charge. Keeping her stance aggressive but controlled, she jutted her chin toward him and leaned ever so slightly in his direction.

"Absolutely not." Then she realized her hand was on the butt of her sidearm. *Oops.* With conscious effort, she loosened her grip and hooked her thumb in her belt. She'd be cool, calm, efficient, with a detached sense of control. She could send out those vibes. Absolutely. Because this man did not make her think of kissing those full lips of his even if she was wondering whether they were soft or firm. No. She would not go there.

She was a professional. On duty. She didn't have time to picture running her fingers through that messy hair of his. Or—or… Her gaze rose from his mouth, quirking up at the corners as it was, to meet his eyes. They really were the soft blue of a star sapphire. She curled her fingers against her belt. Would the stubble on his face be rough, or as soft as his hair looked?

"Darlin', you really shouldn't look at a man that way." His gruff voice was both a caress and a wake-up call.

Quin barely controlled a full-body shudder. She needed to think of ice baths and blizzards. Snow and ski slopes. Invigorating high mountain air. Not warm. Not sexy. She took that step back, both physically and mentally. He laughed, and the sound was dark and warm like fudge brownies just out of the oven. Her mouth watered.

Coffee. She needed coffee. And fresh air. Like right this minute. She squared her shoulders and glanced

at her watch: 4:18 a.m. Despite Quin's hoping otherwise, the DHS worker likely wouldn't arrive until after
sunup.

"It appears we will be here a while, Mr.—"

"Deke."

"Tate. Is there any chance you have coffee hiding
somewhere in this place?"

He chuckled, and she didn't like the way his eyes
crinkled at the corners. No. She didn't like that at all.

"I'll see what I can scare up." He turned away from
her and she realized she needed what cops laughingly
called a 10-100.

"I also…" She did not want to ask, especially when
he turned around, leaned up against the counter by
bracing his hips against it and looked at her.

"You also…?" He did that smile-and-dimple thing
again.

"May I use your facilities?"

"My…" His eyes twinkled and she could tell he was
fighting laughter. The big jerk. "Bathroom is that way."

"Thank you," she acknowledged stiffly. Marching
past him, she made note of the six curtained bunks lining the hall between the living space and the bedroom
she could see at the rear.

Just past the bunk area, through a wooden door,
she walked into a bathroom that made the one in her
condo look like it belonged in a cheap motel. There
was a huge glassed-in shower, a marble countertop
with sink and full-sized commode. It was luxurious.
She closed the door for privacy.

When she was done, she washed her hands and let

her curiosity get the best of her. She poked her head into the bedroom. The queen-size bed appeared to be on a platform. It was higher off the floor than she'd first thought. A pewter-colored comforter looked warm and inviting. Then she stopped to wonder how many women had been in that bed. Time to make a right turn into the sanity lane.

A chair sat in one corner. A guitar occupied a metal stand and there was a microphone in its own stand on the opposite side of the chair. Did he record back here? There was a computer setup on the nearby desk.

Quin heard a throat clearing behind her and she whirled. Her face flaming, she met Deacon's amused gaze without blinking.

"See anything you like, darlin'?"

"Uh…no. Not at all. I was curious to see how the other half lives. That's all."

"Sure." That twinkle in Deacon's eyes had turned to a hard glitter. He stalked toward her.

Self-preservation made her back up, taking one step for each of his. The backs of her legs smacked into the bed and she almost went down—would have hit the mattress if Deacon hadn't reached out and grabbed her arm.

All but panting, Quin forced herself to calm down. She was embarrassed at being caught. She truly hadn't meant to snoop. Much. And then there was the proximity of Deacon—with his dark good looks, the smoldering gleam in his eyes and that mouth. She couldn't help staring at it.

"You're starin' again."

She gulped. Jerking her eyes upward, she attempted to inhale around the catch in her chest. It just wasn't fair to women that one man could be this…everything a man was supposed to be. "Oh. Uh…the coffee?"

"It's ready."

"Oh, good. Great. Yes, thanks. Thank you. Very much." She eased past him and fled toward the living area. She almost stumbled when Deacon called after her, his voice gruff, which invited all sorts of sexy thoughts.

"We're not done, Trooper Kincaid. Not by a long shot."

Four

Deacon fell into bed just before 7:00 a.m. While he appreciated all the help from the Barron wives—or the Bee Dubyas as his brothers called them—they'd exhausted him and Noelle. The baby had been passed around so much she was wailing before he could convince them to go home. It helped that he'd sent out a group text to their husbands to come get them.

But they'd worked some serious magic on short notice. He'd come home to a functional nursery, courtesy of the chain store that was open 24/7. His home was now filled with bottles, diapers, formulas and more clothes than a kid needed in the short term. The crib and playpen thingy were up and ready—not that any of the women put Noelle down long enough for the baby to use them. They'd also set up a baby monitor. As tired as he was, that was a good thing.

Noelle took thirty minutes to calm down. He'd put her in the crib then sat next to it, stroking her gently and singing to her until she fell asleep. Deke had fond memories of singing Dillon to sleep and he sometimes wondered if that was why they both ended up in the music business. In the end, Noelle had been clutching his finger as her eyes drifted shut and her breathing turned into little puffs. He was in desperate need of at least a couple of hours of sleep. Then he'd deal with the curveball life had thrown him—and the intriguing Highway Patrol trooper he'd left in the Thunder River Casino parking lot as she attempted to placate the DHS caseworker.

Bacon. Deacon inhaled deeply. That *was* bacon he was smelling. And biscuits. What the…? He jumped out of bed and stumbled toward the kitchen. He was halfway down the hallway when his brain caught up with his body. The baby-monitor receiver on his bedside table had been turned off. He backtracked to the baby's room and looked in. Noelle was sleeping soundly.

By the time he reached the kitchen, he'd corralled the panic and was mostly coherent. Until he recognized the woman standing at his stove. He should have known she'd come as soon as word leaked out.

"Mom, why are you in my kitchen?"

She leveled him with a look insinuating he was both

not too bright and maybe not her son as a result of that fact.

"Beyond the obvious, Mom."

She poured him a cup of coffee and placed it on the island. He hitched his butt onto one of the bar stools and gratefully accepted her peace offering.

"Your brothers and cousins are in quite the tizzy, son."

Okay. *Son* was better than his full name, but not by much. "It was a crazy night, Mom."

"Uh-huh." She flipped the strips of bacon in the cast-iron frying pan.

"It was late, Mom. Or early, depending on which side of dawn you went to bed."

"Uh-huh."

"Cut me some slack here."

"Don't get snippy, Deacon. Is she yours?"

He studied the steam rising from his mug. "You've seen her."

"Yes."

"What do you think?"

"I think she's a darlin' little girl that somebody— preferably her parents—should love beyond all things."

"We're doing the swabs for the test this afternoon. Chance says it'll take about three weeks. While it's possible, I'm not sure she's mine."

"I figured, sugar. She could be, but I don't think she is, either. As disappointing as that is."

"Mo-o-o-o-m," he warned by stretching out the word.

"None of you are married, Deke, so I am not advocating any of you rush out and find…what's the term you young people use? Baby momma? No baby mommas. Your daddy and I raised you boys to be honorable men, to do the right thing. You'll find the right girl, marry her and *then* have babies. Until we get the paternity-test results, the baby needs looking after. We'll hope her momma decides to come back. 'Course, if she's yours, she's ours. But that's a whole different situation. On the chance she *is* yours, we'll look after her."

Deke slid off the stool, walked around the island to his mom and kissed her on the cheek. "Yeah, we will. So…is that why you decided to come over and fix breakfast for me?" He noted the pile of bacon and sausage patties, the cartons of eggs and the huge pan of homemade biscuits baking in the oven.

"I suspect the locusts will descend soon enough. You know how crazy the family went over Cord's little CJ. Noelle is a baby. That just trips switches like you wouldn't believe."

Except he would, because seeing the baby, hearing her cry and holding her? Yup, every last one of his switches had been tripped. "She might not be mine, Mom."

"If she isn't, what happens if her momma doesn't come back?"

And that was the elephant in the room, wasn't it? "I truly don't know."

"What's your gut say?"

"I brought her home, Mom. No way was I letting her go into the system. But to make a commitment lasting the rest of my life?" He stared out the window over the sink. The note claimed he was Noelle's father. Why didn't the mother confront him? Ask for support? Why hadn't she contacted him before the baby was born? So many questions and no answers. At least not until the DNA test. If the baby wasn't his and they didn't locate her mother, he had no clue what he'd do. "I just don't know, Mom."

"You were always my homebody, Deke. At least until you picked up a guitar. If you weren't out there singin' for your supper every night, you'd be right here with a sweet woman making babies for me to spoil."

He splorted coffee through his nose. She clapped him on the back, pounding a little harder than necessary, and passed him a dish towel to wipe up the mess he'd made.

"Mom, you do remember that I'm the one who took three different girls to prom. The *same* prom."

She scowled at him. "I'm not likely to forget. You were a sophomore and they were seniors."

Deacon coughed behind the towel. He'd also escorted two seniors his junior year, and another three his senior year. Going steady was a foreign concept to him. Heck, the likelihood of his dating a woman more than a couple of times in a row ranked right up there with the Cubs winning the World Series. He'd had one relationship with another country singer that was sort of exclusive and it had ended amicably with both parties going their separate ways. One gossip columnist had labeled him a serial dater. He enjoyed all sorts of women and sex was just gravy.

His mom pointed her finger at him. If there was one deadly thing about Katherine Barron Tate, it was when she brought her "mother finger" to bear on her unruly sons.

Luckily, her lecture was interrupted by a perfunctory knock on the front door followed by the entrance of his older brother, Cooper.

"I smell food!" His brother paused at the door to kick off his muddy boots. "Sorry I missed the concert, little bro. We had a situation on one of the wells last night." Cooper worked with Cord Barron at BarEx, the oil-and-gas exploration-and-energy corporation controlled by the Barrons.

Coop padded into the kitchen and kissed their mother on the cheek. "Mornin', Momma. Sure could use a cup of coffee."

"Is your arm broken? You know where the mugs are kept and the pot is right there staring you in the face."

Laughing, Cooper made himself at home. This was the way of the Tates. There were times Deke wished for boundaries but his big, boisterous family refused to acknowledge them. Before his mother finished the bacon and started a batch of scrambled eggs with onions and peppers, along with home fries, his younger brothers, Bridger and Dillon, had tromped in. The rest of his brothers were likely out of town—Hunter and Boone working with Senator Clay Barron in Washington, DC, and Tucker out in Las Vegas with Chase Barron.

Dillon set the big farm-style table without being asked while Bridger stirred the gravy. Cooper had ducked out to grab a shower, seeing as he was cov-

ered in dirt and grease. When he returned, he was
wearing a pair of Deacon's jeans and a Sons of Nashville concert sweatshirt.

Noelle's whimper echoed from the baby monitor on
the counter, and Deke led the charge. Halfway down
the hallway, he turned to glower, noting how his mother
and Dillon hadn't followed. He grinned evilly. "Coop,
you and Bridge go grab her. I'll get her bottle ready."
At their eager nods of agreement, he began to head
back to the kitchen, then added, "Oh, she'll need a
fresh diaper."

Then he ran, laughing. But between the two of them,
they got Noelle sorted out and appeared with her several minutes later in the kitchen. His mother took over
the care and feeding of the baby while her "boys" ate
their breakfast.

Quin was supposed to be starting her days off. She'd
hit Troop A's headquarters building an hour after her
shift change. She'd spent another hour filling out her
report and filing it so the information would go up
the chain. Whatever was to be done about baby Noelle "Doe" and Deacon Tate was above her pay grade.

Sneaking out the back door after stuffing the report
in her supervisor's in-box, she wanted only home, a
hot shower, a protein shake and bed. In that order. And
when she woke up, she'd have shopping to do. House-
cleaning. Laundry. All the mundane things that normal people did on their days off.

Two hours after she'd arrived home, her supervisor called, jerking her from a sound sleep. She was

to report for duty as soon as she could get to Troop A headquarters.

So…

Here she was, rapping her knuckles on the lieutenant's office door and peeking in through the glass window. He was on the phone but he crooked two fingers and gestured for her to enter. Quin slipped inside and sank onto a chair.

Lieutenant Charles had one of the best poker faces in the Department of Public Safety. As hard as she tried, Quin couldn't get a read on the conversation or who he was talking to, until he ended the call. "Of course, Governor. Whatever we can do to assist."

Her brain went down all sorts of rabbit holes. The governor had lots of reasons to be calling the Oklahoma Highway Patrol, but direct contact with her supervisor at Troop A? It wasn't like he was in the chain of command at the state level. Not that she was paranoid or anything, but after last night, the idea of a political target located between her shoulder blades didn't seem all that far-fetched.

The lieutenant's opening salvo just confirmed her suspicions. "So, you had quite the Friday night."

"You have my report, sir."

"Ease down, Kincaid. Yes. I have your report. And multiple calls from the governor on down." His dry chuckle did little to settle her nerves. "The decision has been made to take you off regular patrol—" He held up his hand, palm facing her to stay the retort she'd opened her mouth to make. "Priorities, Kincaid. And this case is now yours. You'll be the DPS liaison with all the other law-enforcement entities involved. Basically, you're heading up a task force to locate the baby's biological mother, to expedite the investigation and to act as the bridge between law enforcement and Deacon Tate."

"Bridge? What does that mean?"

"That means you are to stay on top of him—"

Quin all but sputtered as her mind went places it had no business going, and all her feminine parts perked right up at the thought.

"And this investigation. You'll work in conjunction with Child Protective Services from the Department of Human Services. The assigned CPS social worker will contact you. There is to be no direct contact with Mr. Tate unless you are present."

The cop side of her brain finally overrode the rest. "Wait. What does that mean, exactly?"

"What it means—exactly—is that you need to work closely with Mr. Tate. He is not to be disturbed by CPS or any law-enforcement agency involved in this investigation. You're point, Kincaid. You take any questions directly to him."

Quin stared, working hard to keep her mouth from gaping. She finally uttered, "Are you kidding me?"

"This is not something to kid about."

"But—"

"No *buts*."

"Yes, there is a *but*, sir. I'm scheduled for vacation time next month."

"Then you better get busy and find the mother, determine if Mr. Tate is the biological father and round up any other pertinent information."

She sat there, staring, her brain emitting nothing but white noise as it tried to wrap itself around the situation.

"Dismissed, Kincaid."

Quin rose, pivoted and headed for the door. The lieutenant's voice stopped her just as her hand touched the knob.

"FYI, Kincaid. No leaks. If any information beyond what DPS releases about this investigation gets out, it's all on your head."

Her mouth felt numb, just like her semicoherent brain, but she muttered, "Yes, sir," then exited. But the lieutenant still wasn't done.

"You need to get out to Mr. Tate's ranch and talk to him, Kincaid. Welfare check on the baby and all that. ASAP."

Oh, whoop-de-do. She had plans for today and none of them included driving to Timbuktu to deal with a spoiled star. Except there was a baby involved and seriously, what single guy was truly capable of 24/7 child care?

First, she had to locate directions. Then she'd just *drop in* on the man himself. And give him a piece of her mind.

Five

When Quin pulled up in front of Deacon Tate's gorgeous log home, she found a driveway full of vehicles. She parked at the end of the line and trudged past a dark-colored Dodge Challenger. She noted the manufacturer's badges. It was an SRT Hellcat HEMI muscle car—a model that cost almost as much as she made in a year.

The next vehicle was far less flashy—a black Ford Expedition, platinum edition. A white four-wheel-drive Ford F-250 pickup with the emblem for Barron Exploration plastered on the door was parked close to the walkway leading to the front door. Next to it was a Lexus LX 570, its metallic pearl-white paint almost blinding in the bright winter sun.

So much for confronting Tate alone. Quin marched

up the fieldstone walkway and stopped at the double-wide wooden doors. She looked but couldn't find a doorbell, nor was there a door knocker—just a numeric keypad. Using the heel of her fist, she banged on the door.

A muffled voice called from inside. She pounded the door again. And waited. She had her hand on the handle when the door was jerked open. Off balance, she fell into a hard body. Muscular arms gripped Quin's waist, steadying her. Heat spread from strong fingers, radiating through her Kevlar vest to tease her skin.

She looked up into a pair of star-sapphire eyes and got a little lost in their mysterious depths.

"Don't just stand there, Deacon," a woman's voice ordered. "Let the poor girl in."

"Certainly." A boyish grin teased his mouth, and Quin's heart did a funny little flutter kick. "Please come in, Trooper Kincaid. We were just having breakfast. Are you hungry?"

She was so focused on his mouth that her brain went to the one place she didn't want it to go. She blinked to break the spell he'd cast. Quin once again considered the effect this man had on his female fans, and she frowned at the thought of the lingerie collection he and his bandmates probably laughed about.

"Quin?"

"I'm not hungry."

"Of course you are, hon. Come on in and sit. I'll get you a plate." The feminine voice came from inside the house and wasn't asking.

Quin watched Deacon walk through the large open

living area toward a fabulous kitchen. Like the rest of
the house, it looked as if it should be the centerfold in
a decorating magazine.

"Don't dawdle, hon. Food's gettin' cold."

As Quin trailed in Deacon's wake, she studied the
other people gathered around a granite island that
looked big enough to land a small plane on. There
were three men, two of whom she recognized from
the previous night, and an older woman. The family
resemblance was strong.

Deacon stopped at one of the bar stools and pulled
it out for her. She settled on it and a plate heaped with
bacon, sausages and eggs appeared in front of her.
Deacon snagged flatware and a napkin—cloth—for
her use.

"Share the biscuits and gravy, Cooper," the woman
said. "I'm Katherine Tate. I take it you've met my sons
Deacon and Dillon. These are two of my other sons,
Cooper and Bridger. Coffee or something else t'drink?"

Her head was spinning a little. "Oh, coffee, please."

"Cream or sugar?"

She glanced at the oldest of the men present, though
he wasn't *old*. Quin guessed him to be in his midthir-
ties. "A little sugar, please, and vanilla creamer if you
have it." She offered a tight smile to the men's mother.
"Nice to meet you, Mrs. Tate. I'm Quincy Kincaid. I've
been assigned by OHP as liaison on this case."

Katherine's eyes narrowed. "Case? This isn't a case,
Miz Kincaid. This is a little girl. Who has a name."
At that moment, a soft mewl issued from a soft-sided
criblike thing Quin hadn't noticed upon her arrival.

"I'll get the baby, Deacon. Finish your breakfast before it gets cold. And take your hat off, Miz Kincaid."

Quin removed her hat and set it on the stool next to her. Ignoring the stares from Deacon's brothers, she concentrated on the food in front of her. She forked eggs into her mouth and chewed carefully. The silence filling the room was so thick she could have been wearing earplugs. She couldn't even hear the four men breathing and that was saying something.

The stalemate broke when Katherine Tate returned, the baby slung easily on one hip. Quin supposed that after seven sons, Mrs. Tate would have had lots of practice with infants. Transfixed, she watched as Deacon's mother did a sort of slinking, rocking walk toward them. The woman was suddenly right there standing between her and Deacon.

"Here." Mrs. Tate thrust the baby forward and Quin braced for it, figuring she was meant to be the recipient. But Deacon's mom passed Noelle to him. Feeling idiotic, Quin let her arms fall to her sides and swiveled to stare at her plate.

"She's clean. I'll fix her another bottle but you feed her this time. Eat fast."

"Yes, ma'am," Deke muttered around a mouthful of biscuit.

"Don't talk with your mouth full."

"Yes, ma'am." This time his voice was clear, his mouth empty.

Quin was fascinated. These men were all adults—well, all but Dillon maybe. He looked like a big man-child and she suspected that since he was the baby, he got away with everything. But it didn't matter that they were grown and held impressive jobs; this woman owned them. Then again, it was rather cute the way they got all goofy and treated her with respect. They weren't like Quin's brothers in any way, shape or form. Then again, she and her siblings hadn't grown up in the lap of luxury like the Tates.

Deacon scraped the last bite of eggs and potatoes off his plate, chewed vigorously and swallowed. She couldn't take her eyes off his mouth or his throat. And she was impressed by the way he had the baby propped up on his lap and was holding her so confidently in the crook of his left arm.

Mrs. Tate handed the bottle and a clean dish towel to Deacon. "I'll clear your plate. Go feed our little girl."

"You sure you don't wanna feed her, Mom?"

The woman looked aghast and wagged her index finger in his direction. "I only fed her this mornin' because you hadn't had your coffee, Deacon. I did my time with the seven of you. You're on your own now."

Quin stiffened when she realized Mrs. Tate was staring at her, the look in the older woman's eyes speculative. She slid off the stool and picked up her plate to carry it…somewhere. The sink?

"Just leave it, hon. Coop and Bridge are on dish duty."

The two brothers groaned but it was a good-natured sound, and Dillon gloated. His mother pointed at him. "You need to go get the trash in the nursery and take it out."

"Aw, Mom," Dillon protested.

She leveled a look at him that made Quin straighten her spine and bite her tongue to keep from offering to do it just so the woman would stop glaring.

"Quin?" Deacon called to her.

Whew. A reprieve. She hurried into the great room and stood near the large leather chair Deacon occupied. Noelle was draining her bottle with vigorous sucking noises. This was Quin's chance to tell him what was going to happen and then leave. "Do you have a moment to talk? We have to get some things straight."

He arched a brow and nodded toward the end of the couch nearest his chair. "So talk."

Quin settled herself on the couch, cognizant of being the focus of attention—*everyone's* attention. "As I mentioned when I arrived, I'm the law-enforcement liaison in this case. We've started the investigation into the baby's circumstances. Once we locate the mother—"

"Do you think you will?"

"Will what?"

Deacon glanced down to hide his grin. He enjoyed knocking the stodgy trooper off balance. She had a script and every time he threw her off, she got flustered. He liked the color in her cheeks and the snap of blue fire in her eyes when she got angry.

"Find Noelle's mother."

"Of course we will. It's just a matter of time. Then DHS will do an evaluation and a determination will be made taking into account the results of the paternity test."

"You think she's unfit because she left Noelle with

me." Okay, maybe he shouldn't have sounded so accusatory but something in Quin's tone rankled.

"That's not up to me to decide."

"But you have."

"Look, Mr. Tate—"

"Deacon."

"Mr. Tate." She glowered. "The woman left her baby out in the cold next to your tour bus claiming you are the father." She studied him through narrow eyes. "Though there might be a possibility you're the father, pending the test results, we just don't know. What I don't understand is why a single man, and a—a…" She waved one hand and bit out the next words like they tasted bitter. "A rich superstar would insist on accepting custody of a baby that might not be his."

Noelle started sucking air. Deke pulled the empty bottle away, settled her on his shoulder and patted her back until she burped loudly. He pushed out of the chair and stared down at Quin. "It appears that Noelle's mother knows me better than you do."

Cuddling the infant against his shoulder, Deke walked to the kitchen and settled on the bar stool he'd vacated earlier. Noelle was cooing and nuzzling against his neck. He was ticked off at Quin and her preconceived notions. What she thought she knew about him was obviously gleaned from scandal rags and cheesy entertainment shows on TV. He should just ignore the irritation but something inside him really wanted this woman to like him.

Yeah, fat chance of that.

His mother brushed past him, pausing a moment

to whisk hair out of his eyes, the gesture both oddly endearing and annoying. He watched her roost on the couch next to Quin, looking every inch a Southern matriarch. His mom wore jeans, Western boots and a turtleneck sweater, but from her demeanor, she might as well have been wearing a designer dress and pearls.

The two women began to converse in low voices and Deke couldn't make out what they were saying over the noise his brothers made cleaning up. His mother's gaze danced between him and Quin, which made him a little nervous. Okay, it made him a lot nervous. Katherine Tate was a plotter, especially where her boys were concerned.

Thinking to tell his brothers to keep it down, he glanced around just in time to see Bridger nudge Cooper's shoulder.

"If I ever catch Mom lookin' at me the way she's lookin' at Deke, especially with a pretty woman in the room, I'm headin' for the hills."

Cooper grinned. "Smart man. I'd be right behind you."

"So what are we gonna do?" Bridger glanced at Coop.

"Sit back and enjoy the show." Cooper tossed his dish towel over his shoulder and leaned against the counter, crossing his ankles and arms.

"Y'all know I can hear you, right?" Deke scowled at them.

His brothers burst out laughing. Dillon, approaching the back door and holding a plastic bag at arm's length, jerked his head around. "What's so funny? What'd I miss?"

"You're too young to understand," Cooper teased.

"Seriously? You're going to pull that crap on me now?" Dillon waved the sack to emphasize his point then gave Deke a sideways glance. "They're right about one thing. She is pretty. Think she'd go out with me?"

Bridger smirked. "Naw. You're too young for her."

"Hey, I'm twenty-two. I'm right at the peak of my sex—"

"You boys do know that Trooper Kincaid and I can hear you, yes?" Katherine didn't need to raise her voice to be heard.

"Yes, ma'am," four voices replied in unison, with Dillon adding, "Well, do you? Because she's really hot."

Bridger rolled his eyes. "Dude, we can't take you anywhere. You do realize that you're bird-dogging the woman our big brother is interested in, right?"

"Not to mention you're a baby," Cooper added. "She wants a real man, not a pimply-faced—"

Dillon shoved Coop. "I don't have pimples!"

Deke wanted to bash all three of his brothers. This was normal behavior anytime two or more Tates shared the same space, but today he needed a huge helping of *regular* normal to deal with the trooper. He couldn't help but wonder what she was thinking. She looked stern in her dark brown uniform and black leather Sam Browne belt, but he caught a hint of humor around her eyes. At least he hoped it was humor. Did she have a boisterous family like his? That would be a good thing. She'd understand the ribbing and his frustration.

"I still think she should go out with me." Dillon was a persistent little bugger.

"Then you think wrong. *She* thinks you're too young," Quin called out. She didn't even look their way but her voice carried.

Was she teasing Dillon? That made Deke feel like a fool because he was suddenly jealous of his little brother. He needed to get some space and think through this situation—and this woman. She was not his type, not in any way, shape or form. Except it was turning out that she was exactly his type in every way, shape and form. He was so screwed.

Six

"Pay no mind to the boys, Quincy." Katherine Tate gave her an inquisitive look. "I may call you Quincy, yes? Trooper Kincaid is so…harsh."

Quin nodded out of habit. Mrs. Tate was one of those women so used to getting her own way she'd likely steamroll over any protestations Quin might make.

"Do you have family, Quincy?"

Mrs. Tate was getting personal now. Quin would have to walk this minefield with care—at least until she figured out the woman's angle.

"Yes, ma'am."

"Brothers?"

"Yes, ma'am."

Mrs. Tate laughed, a rich laugh much like her son's that reminded Quin of hot fudge on ice cream. She wondered what it had been like having this woman as a mother, especially since her own was 180 degrees opposite in personality.

"I shall remind the boys not to play poker with you. Tell me about your brothers. Are you close?"

"No."

"Ah."

Quin squirmed. That one syllable spoke volumes and what it said made her bristle. All teasing aside, she had the distinct impression that she was interviewing for a job.

"My brothers and I weren't particularly close, either. Of course, I often thought Daddy should have drowned Cyrus at birth but then I wouldn't have my nephews so I suppose it all worked out. Families are odd microcosms, don't you think?"

Quin wasn't sure what to say. Cyrus Barron had been a powerful man, not just in Oklahoma, but pretty much in the entire world. His six sons—one only recently acknowledged—were following in his footsteps. The family had fingers in every important pie and then some. She wasn't as familiar with the Tate brothers but knew several of them worked side-by-side with their Barron cousins.

"Yes," Quin finally answered. "They can be." Which was true enough. Odd and dysfunctional described her family rather well.

"How closely do you plan to…*supervise* my son, Trooper Kincaid?"

The abrupt change of subject caught Quin off guard.

"Technically, I'm only here as a liaison, ma'am. A… facilitator, so to speak."

"In other words, the governor called your big boss, who called your immediate boss, who stuck you with this because no one wants to upset the governor. I still want to know your intentions, Quincy. You aren't comfortable with this situation. And you especially don't like the idea of my son taking care of a baby."

Yeah. She'd sure enough poked the momma bear. With a sharp stick. "I admit to reservations, Mrs. Tate, especially given the fact that your son is uncertain whether he's the father."

The only reaction she got was the quirk of a well-shaped brow and silence.

"Look, I'm going to be blunt here. Why would your son take in a child he probably has no ties to? Aren't you worried this is a scam? Some sort of shakedown for money?"

Quin didn't understand why Deacon and his family were making such a big deal over this. Didn't it make more sense to just turn over the kid? She breathed through her irritation and continued. "While we are making every attempt to keep the situation low-key, your son is a celebrity. It's just a matter of time before the story leaks to the media. What happens then? I'm a trained investigator, Mrs. Tate. As such, I have to question your son's motive."

That earned Quin another pointed look. "That explains quite a bit, young lady."

Well, crud. She was losing ground fast and she really needed Mrs. Tate on her side. Quin figured Deacon's mother might be the only person who could make him see reason.

"Be honest with me, Mrs. Tate. Are you really okay with your son taking in this child on a whim?"

"A whim?" Deacon's voice was cold enough to raise goose bumps on her arms. Quin had totally forgotten that he and his brothers were just steps away.

"What would you call it, Mr. Tate?"

Deke glanced at his mother. She had that weird look on her face again, her gaze bouncing between him and Quin like she was watching them play Ping-Pong.

"Compassion, *Trooper* Kincaid, something you seem to be seriously lacking."

When Quin pushed to her feet and went toe-to-toe with him, Deke's anger melted into something hotter. He dropped his gaze to her mouth, watching her talk but not really listening. His brain had taken him right to the heart of what he wanted to do with Quin's mouth. The fantasy was so vivid his hands were reaching for her when he remembered where they were and what was happening. He tuned back just in time, and she said, "Why would a man like you—"

"A man like me?" He folded his arms across his chest. Yeah, there'd be no touching or kissing now. "Care to elaborate?"

Quin sputtered for a moment. Deke was suddenly aware that his brothers had formed a semicircle behind him in a show of solidarity. He'd handed off Noelle to Bridger when the tone of the women's conversation had changed. His mother hadn't moved, but her face was now a blank canvas.

Inhaling, Quin focused on him. "Yes, Mr. Tate. A man like you. A rich man. A…star. Aren't you in the middle of a tour? Why in the world would you want to take on the care and feeding of an infant? I can't help but consider this might be a publicity stunt—a way to boost your media presence."

Deke held on to his temper only because Cooper put his hand on his shoulder and squeezed. Hard. "So…let me get this straight. You think I'm a publicity whore who would use a baby as a way to get on the entertainment news. The bottom line—" he was all but shaking now "—is you believe that because I'm rich there is no way I could be doin' something like this simply because it's the right thing to do."

Quin opened and closed her mouth several times, apparently unable to speak. That worked just fine for Deke. She'd said more than enough, and no matter how sexy she was, he doubted he could get around her preconceived notions. He and his brothers had been raised to work for a living. His daddy would have tanned their hides if they showed even a hint of the attitude this maddening woman was accusing him of having.

"Have I got that right?" He glared at her as he pulled his cell phone out of his hip pocket and dialed Chance. The conversation was short. "I don't care what you have to do but I want Trooper Kincaid removed from the case." With the phone still pressed to his ear, he said to Quin, "Since you've already decided I'm guilty, I'm damned if I do, damned if I don't. Here's the deal—

until Noelle's mother is found, she is mine and I will take care of her."

Chance questioned him on the situation so Deke added, "She accused me of staging a publicity stunt. I want her gone." He cut the call.

"Mr. Tate—"

"I will give you five minutes, Trooper Kincaid. I will show you the nursery that's been set up. I will show you that not only am I capable, but that I *am* taking care of Noelle. Follow me."

Deke stormed off as his brothers quickly cleared out of his way. He glanced back, not to see if Quin was following him, but to check his mother's expression. The woman was smiling. What was up with that? He didn't care, though he probably should. He had enough problems on his hands with the prickly state cop.

His brothers wisely stayed in the great room. When Deke and Quin reached the guest room next to the master bedroom, he stood back and ushered her inside. She'd detoured past the kitchen to snag her Smokey Bear hat and it was perched firmly on her head. Deke noticed the quick cut of her eyes toward the open doorway of his bedroom as she hesitated. He'd spent a portion of his dreams plotting ways to get her into his bed. That had been a complete waste of time.

He followed her into the guest room. The Bee Dubyas had done an amazing job. The queen-size bed had been moved into a corner to make room for the crib. The top of the dresser had been cleared and padded for a changing table. They'd even installed a thing that warmed the baby wipes. The drawers were filled with diapers and baby clothes. Toys dotted the glider chair and the baby monitor—a whole house system—was front and center.

Deke leaned a shoulder against the doorjamb and watched Quin examine the space that had been created literally overnight to accommodate a baby. He had to reach deep to level out his temper. Why should he care if this cop liked him? He was doing the right thing and her opinion shouldn't matter. Yet for some reason it did.

Whoever Noelle's mother was, she was looking for something better for her child. At least he hoped that was her motivation. What did he actually know? Maybe the woman *was* trying to set him up for a paternity suit, which was easily defended with DNA. The baby had been well taken care of, according to Jolie. And she'd come with all the stuff babies came with—diapers, bottles, formula, clothes.

Quin whirled and faced him, her eyes snapping with irritation. "I find it somewhat amazing that you had this cozy little nest all prepared for this baby who isn't yours." She waved a hand around the room. "Especially since you claim ignorance about the existence of this child before last night. When the CPS caseworker comes out for the home study, I'm sure she'll make note of it."

Deacon stiffened and gave her a narrow look. "What caseworker and what home study?"

She closed her eyes, breathed, in an apparent attempt to ratchet down her temper. Deke was almost sorry. Sparring with her was entertaining.

"The state won't just turn over the baby to you.

It doesn't work that way in the real world. I get that you're Mr. Nashville Star and all, but here you have to follow the same rules as everyone else. Doesn't matter who you are. And it doesn't matter which judge signed those papers your cousin had drawn up." She muttered that last part.

Okay, so who would guess the confounding woman was still feeling the sting of Chance's middle-of-the-night call to the judge?

She inhaled and continued. "I just don't understand why a megastar like *Deacon Tate*—who has doubts he's the biological father—would take on the responsibility of a baby."

Deke didn't miss Quin's switch to discussing him in the third person. "Is there a reason you don't like me?"

"What?" Evidently, his question caught her off guard.

"You don't like me. I'd like to know why. If I've done something to offend you or—"

"I don't...*dislike* you."

"But you don't like me, either."

"Look, Mr. Tate, I'm just doing my job. Liking you or not has no bearing."

Deke pushed off the door frame. "We're done here."

Her eyes snapped with temper again. "No, we aren't."

Quin marched up to him and once again, they were toe-to-toe. Her mouth was right there, all plump and glistening because she'd just wet her lips. Was he quick enough to catch that tongue before it disappeared from sight? She leaned toward him and her eyes went a little unfocused. Close. So. Very. Very...

And then they were kissing. It wasn't sweet. It wasn't sensual. It was hard and angry and they each fought to dominate. He cinched his arm around her waist and hauled her up against him. Instead of soft breasts, he encountered stiffness. She was wearing a bulletproof vest? And oh, yeah, she was wearing her weapons belt, complete with pistol. Deke had totally blanked out that she was in uniform. Why was that so freaking sexy?

His free hand knocked her hat off and fisted in the tight bun at the back of her neck. He used his grip to angle her head so he could deepen the kiss. He bit at her bottom lip, tasted her with his tongue. When she sighed, he plunged his tongue into her mouth, tasting her fully now.

Her hands gripped the plackets of his flannel shirt, and it felt like she was both jerking him closer and pushing him away. He didn't care. The only thing that mattered was that they were kissing. Deke watched her, smiled into the kiss as her eyes drifted closed. She wasn't fighting for control now and her surrender was one of the sweetest things he'd ever experienced.

Without considering the consequences, he turned them around, backing Quin up against the wall. His whole being responded to her body pressed against him and he really wanted to strip her out of all that brown. Brown wasn't her color. Naked was. He wanted to touch *her*, not the vest binding her tight. He broke the kiss to nuzzle the soft pulse point under her chin. Her breathing changed rhythm. That was good. He ground his hips against hers, the friction feeling so good against his erection.

"I—"

He cut off whatever she was going to say by kissing her again. She tasted of coffee. She smelled faintly of peaches and cinnamon and his mouth watered. Peach cobbler with ice cream and a cup of steaming coffee. His favorite dessert. At least until he got his mouth on Quin. And he would. He would taste her in all sorts of ways.

"Ahem."

Deke cut his eyes to the door. Wonderful. Dillon stood there grinning like a demented elf. That was when he realized Quin was thumping on his chest with her fists and shaking her head from side to side in an effort to break their kiss. He backed away and was enjoying the heck out of the look he'd put on her face. Her cheeks were rosy, her hair tousled, the bun all but destroyed. Her eyes were half-lidded with desire even as they narrowed in anger. Her lips were swollen and red and she was breathing hard.

He caught the flash of movement from the corner of his eye and just managed to duck out of the way of Quin's fist, aimed for his chest, not his face.

"You are despicable," she hissed before her glower swept across him to include Dillon. She pushed Deke out of her way and shoved past his little brother. Moments later, he heard the door to the guest bathroom close and lock.

"I've heard that about you," Dillon teased. "Definitely despicable."

"Shut up." There was no heat in his voice because, truth be told, he was feeling pretty cocky. He'd upset Quin's equilibrium enough that she hadn't wanted to slap him—she'd wanted to slug him. Perverse, he realized, but it still made him just a little proud he'd gotten to her. And he had definitely gotten to her. She'd been kissing him back just as hard.

By the time he got around Dillon, Quin had cleared the bathroom and he caught sight of her not-quite-tight bun disappearing down the hall. Of course, the sway of her hips in those tan uniform pants made him have to adjust himself as he followed her back to the living room.

Quin didn't pause as she headed straight for the front door. Deke stopped, and that was when Dillon shoved her hat into his hands. He wanted to laugh and wondered how long it would take for the staid trooper to realize she was technically out of uniform. He'd about decided to keep the hat as a souvenir—and an excuse to see her again—when she pulled an about-face, stalked back to him and ripped the hat from his hands.

One of her eyes was twitching, her lips were pursed and bright red spots stained her cheeks. "Not a word," she growled, pivoting and marching toward the door again.

"Trooper Kincaid?" His mother's use of Quin's title stopped her as she reached for the door handle. Her shoulders stiffened and her back went ramrod-straight but she didn't look around.

"Yes?"

"Do you have pearls, dear?"

Seven

Pearls? What did pearls have to do with anything that had just occurred? Seriously? No, Quin didn't have pearls. Did she look like the kind of woman who would wear them? She turned to gape at Mrs. Tate. The woman smiled, waiting expectantly for her answer.

"Um, no, ma'am. No pearls."

"That's a shame, Quincy. Every woman should have pearls handy when she needs something to clutch. Do drive safely back to the city."

And just like that, Quincy had been dismissed. What was up with this family? Oh, yeah. They were rich and they could pretty much do whatever they wanted. Except she wouldn't let them get away with this—whatever *this* was.

She stewed all the way back to Oklahoma City—

over the situation and her reaction to Deacon. Quincy couldn't relate to the Tates. She needed to understand the motivations behind Deacon's alleged altruism. Cause and effect. Incentives. Reasons. What were they? Granted, her family wasn't any sort of benchmark but there had to be a payoff in it for Deacon. But what could it be?

She'd asked similar questions as a child when she'd been plucked out of her group home to spend Christmas with a rich family. Their mansion had been full of Christmas decorations with a big tree and lots of presents. A TV station even did a story. Quin figured she'd hit the jackpot until the day after Christmas. The family sent her back to the group home. She didn't get to keep any of the presents the TV camera filmed her opening.

Yeah, in her jaded experience, people—especially the wealthy—didn't do something for nothing.

Quincy was no closer to answers for any of her questions when she parked in front of her apartment. She could write her report—and wouldn't it be a doozy— and email it to the LT. Then she could finally get around to the other things she'd scheduled for her day off.

She was in line at the grocery store when her phone dinged—a message from the lieutenant. Quincy was still on the hook—a welfare check tomorrow and every day thereafter. So much for Deacon or Chance Barron getting her kicked off the case. Darn it. She kept reading. Her recommendation to call in DHS was under advisement and the baby was to stay where she was. Quin also needed to locate the mother ASAP.

Great. Just…great.

Days off were rescinded to be made up in comp time. Still, the sooner she found the mother, the sooner she could get her life back. She had time to close this case before boarding her plane for those two glorious weeks far, far away. Time to put her investigative skills to work.

Deacon stared at five of his cousins. Thank goodness Clay and his wife, Georgie, were still in DC. The rest of the Barrons—and their wives—had descended first thing Sunday morning, including Chase and Savannah, who'd flown in from Vegas. At the moment, the women were passing Noelle around and cooing over the baby like she was a porcelain doll. The men were staring back at him, their expressions bleak.

"What?" He sounded defensive.

"A baby? Seriously?" Chase cut his eyes to his wife, who was currently rocking Noelle. "What are you tryin' to do to us, cuz?"

"I've heard nothing but 'baby, baby, baby' since Friday night." Cord scrubbed his forehead with the heel of his hand. "CJ is all 'I want a brother, Dad.' And Jolie? She's got that look in her eye." He shuddered dramatically. "I'm just now getting used to being the dad of a real kid."

Chance laughed. "As opposed to a fake kid?"

"You know what I mean," Cord grumbled. "Babies don't talk. Or play ball. Or *do* stuff." He eyed the women. "And I'm betting Cassie is giving you the same pitch as the rest of the wives."

Lifting his shoulders in a philosophical shrug, Chance said, "I figure they can all get their baby fix hanging out over here."

Forgotten in the banter, Deacon growled under his breath. He didn't want these daily invasions. Okay, granted, it was sort of nice to take a break from the constant vigilance of watching over Noelle, but he'd scheduled this time at home to get away from crowds and people. He'd hoped to write some songs, to ride— though that was on the back burner now—and just hang out at the one place that gave him peace. Thank goodness none of *his* brothers was married; otherwise he'd have no time alone.

Cash poured another cup of coffee for himself. "Roxie treats that damn dog of hers like a kid. I think I'm safe for a while."

Nudging his twin, Chase laughed. "You love that dog as much as she does, Cash."

"Shhh. She doesn't need to know that. And I figure as soon as Pippa pops, they'll all have a new baby to fuss over." Cash winked at Kade before turning his gaze toward Deke. "So, you want Barron Security to look into the situation?"

Deke nodded. Cash was the one cousin he really wanted to speak to. "Yeah. There's not much to go on and that trooper is supposed to be investigating. Knowing the governor, the Oklahoma Statue Bureau of Investigation is probably involved, too. I'll keep Noelle until you find the mom. Then we'll figure things out from there."

"What happens if Cash doesn't find her?" Chance asked. "Have you thought about the future?"

Deke pursed his lips, considering his answer. He hadn't shaken the thoughts of settling down and starting a family that had been floating in his brain just prior to finding the baby. Not that he believed in karma or the universe dropping a big ol' sign like a baby on him, but he still wondered at the timing. The munchkin had been in his life not even forty-eight hours, yet he couldn't imagine not hearing her sleepy sounds through the monitor, not filling his nose with the sweet scent inherent to babies. Well, as long as they were dry. He chuckled.

"I can't honestly say, Chance. Keeping her would mean a lot of changes. I'd need to hire a nanny because I'm not an idiot. With my schedule, there's no way I could be a full-time single dad. After New Year's, we go back to touring for a couple of months. Then we plan to take time off, work on the new album. I could be here."

"You aren't seriously considering keeping this child, are you?" Chance's eyes narrowed and he looked like he was ready to launch into a lecture consisting of all the reasons it was a bad idea.

"I don't know, Chance." Deke held up his hand to stall further comment. "I'm aware of all the negatives. Trust me. And remember, I am not an idiot, despite what y'all, my brothers and my mom seem to think. Best-case scenario, the mother turns up soon, and we

can help her through whatever it is that made her leave
Noelle on the bus. Christmas is coming. I'm betting
she—"

"There are other considerations," Cash interrupted.
He glanced at Chance and got a slight nod in reply.
"What if this is a setup? We can't ignore any ulterior
motives the mother might have."

"I'm aware of that, too. That's why I'd rather you
track her down and we figure out what her deal is before the cops do."

Cash nodded, exchanging another look with Chance,
but it was Chase who spoke up. "I'll have our PR people work on damage control—"

"Chase—"

"Just in case, Deke. Let Cash do his job and let me
do mine while waiting on results of the test. As family, we only have your best interest at heart."

The doorbell rang. Roxie popped up off the floor to
answer it. The men sitting around the kitchen island
swiveled their heads to see who had arrived.

"Speaking of best interests…" Kade, heretofore silent, waggled his brows suggestively.

Quin was startled by the redhead who opened the
door. There'd been a whole new fleet of vehicles in the
drive as she arrived; she should have suspected that
Deacon's harem would show up. She wasn't expecting so many women, though. Then her brain kicked
into gear. These weren't fangirls. No, that would have
been too simple. She was facing the very formidable
Barron wives.

"May I help you?" the redhead asked, one brow arched. She obviously wasn't expecting Quin.

"That's just the nanny state checking up on me, Roxie." Deacon's voice wafted above the sudden silence.

Roxie Barron. Quin put name and face together. Roxanne Rowland had married Cash Barron of Barron Security earlier in the year. Quin had done her homework and was finally matching names, faces and spouses. Roxie had been at the casino Friday night. Stepping around her, Quin stopped at the edge of the living area. The women were spread over the couches and chairs while the men were gathered in the kitchen. Odd, until she realized the baby was in the living room. She had to stifle a laugh.

The women fawned over the baby while the men huddled together, like there was strength in numbers, as far away from the kid as they could get. Quin couldn't help but wonder if there would be a Barron baby boom a year from now. She fixed her gaze on Deacon. He didn't look any happier to see her than she was to see him. She lowered her eyes the moment she recognized the heat in his. Warmth climbed up her neck, flushing her cheeks. She'd counted on his anger, in light of his instructions to Chance Barron, but this flare of desire between them knocked her off balance.

The tingling in her lips and the quivers lower in her body didn't help matters. Of all the guys she'd come across in her life, why did it have to be this one that got her thinking about monkey business instead of her job? She had nothing against men or dating, it was just that most of the ones she came in contact with weren't suitable because they were candidates for arrest, or they were put off by her job. The last thing she wanted or needed was to get involved with a spoiled star with daddy dilemmas.

"As you can see, Trooper Kincaid, Noelle is fine and being spoiled rotten. Last time I checked the state statutes, spoiling a baby wasn't a felony."

She caught a twinkle in his eye. Was he flirting with her?

"No, just a misdemeanor, and bad parenting," Quin wanted to bite her tongue. She was not flirting back.

"Ah, I see. Good thing my attorney is present." His mouth quirked. He *was* flirting with her.

"He seems to be everywhere you are. That makes you a suspicious subject." She couldn't stop her response, even as she dug the hole deeper.

"Does that mean I'm a person of…interest?"

Quin curled her lips between her teeth to keep from answering. Innuendo dripped off his words. They weren't flirting. Really they weren't. Flirting with Deacon Tate was a bad thing, especially after that kiss—the one she was desperate to forget. She blinked and discovered he was halfway across the room, headed her direction.

"Suddenly at a loss for words, Trooper?" He was right there, inches from her face. Everything feminine in her body perked right up. This man punched all the right tickets and she wanted to take the ride. Except she couldn't afford the complications.

"A smart person only speaks when there's something worthwhile to say."

Deacon leaned in and whispered, "Oh, I have plenty to say, Trooper Kincaid. And not just with words."

She shivered, a reflex from his warm breath in her ear. Thank goodness she was wearing Kevlar because her chest brushed his and without the vest, Deacon would know exactly what he was doing to her. Working to control her expression, she leaned back so she could see his face. In doing so, she caught a glimpse of everyone else. Ten people were staring at Deacon like he'd grown two heads.

Deacon struggled to control his breathing and his desire. He wanted to take her into his arms. Or back her against the wall. Again. He wanted to taste her mouth. Again. And he wanted to do a whole lot more. Except they had an audience. How had he forgotten that? His cousins needed to leave. Right now. And Noelle needed a long nap. Immediately. And he definitely needed to get Quincy out of her uniform and into his bed.

Which was not the brightest idea he'd ever had. The woman obviously didn't like him—or his family. She seemed convinced he couldn't handle Noelle, that the baby would be better off in foster care. That wasn't happening. Despite their differences, he couldn't deny his attraction to her. She was…tough. Forceful. Strong. Beautiful. And sexy beyond belief.

They stood there, staring at each other, both of them breathing hard. Was she remembering the feel of his mouth on hers? Of their bodies pressed together? He was so hard he worried his zipper might break. Walking across the room had been torture and he hoped no one noticed the obvious. Standing close and breathing in her peach-cobbler scent left him throbbing.

One of his cousins whistled a tune Deke recognized—Jason Aldean's "Burnin' It Down." As much as he wanted to be alone with Quincy, it was best they had chaperones—even smart-alecky ones. The last thing he should do was get involved with the cop investigating Noelle's abandonment. He stepped back, which was harder than he'd anticipated.

"Why exactly are you here again?" Deke asked, focusing on business, not pleasure.

"I've been ordered to make a daily welfare check." She sounded breathless, if officious.

"As you can see, Noelle is once again healthy, happy, fed and clean. Is there anything else, Trooper Kincaid?" He smiled slightly, figuring his dimple was putting a punctuation mark on the smirk.

"Look, Deacon, I don't want to traipse out here every day any more than you want me here."

"You're wrong there, darlin'. You have no idea what I want." He liked the way her eyes widened at his declaration as her cheeks turned pink again.

"I am not your *darlin'*." She did a decent impersonation of his voice.

"Yet."

"Ever." Her eyes got all squinty and her mouth scrunched up. The expression was so exasperated and cute it was all Deke could do to keep from kissing her right then and there. "*Argh.* Don't even," she threatened, backing away from him, one hand reaching back for the door.

"Same time tomorrow, darlin'?" He stepped toward her, grabbing for the door as she ducked away.

The door slammed shut.

Eight

Deke hadn't meant to slam the door. Really. The wind caught it and pulled it shut. Well, that was his story and he'd stick to it as he turned around and faced ten pairs of eyes. Eleven if he counted Noelle's. Except hers were screwed up tight and her mouth was open for a mighty wail. He was all too familiar with that expression but he knew how to preempt the crying jag.

He waded through the wives, plucked the baby from Jolie's arms and kept walking. Noelle's impending tears were a good excuse to hide away from his nosy family. He settled in the big, wooden rocking chair he'd installed in the makeshift nursery. Crooning a song and rocking always worked on the baby girl.

Deke had about ten minutes of peace before the

door eased open. He was surprised to see Kade standing there.

"You draw the short straw?" Deke kept his voice soft and slightly singsong.

His cousin, only recently acknowledged as one of the late Cyrus Barron's sons, ducked his head to hide a grin.

"Naw. They probably don't even know I'm gone. That said, once you get out there, the questions are gonna fly. That trooper hit the radar of every wife and your reaction didn't exactly go unnoticed. Is there something we should know?"

Deke made a face, and Kade held up both hands in front of him, backing up a step. "Not my business. Got it. And it's not really the reason I'm here. I know you aren't running much livestock these days, but now that you're caring for the baby, if you need help, all you have to do is call. It's not like you have a wife or babysitter to leave Noelle with while you work down at the barn."

"Good point, but my foreman lives on the ranch. He'll cover everything until Christmas and then he's taking his family to Texas for the holidays. As long as the weather stays good, I can put her in—" Deke looked around "—something. That carrier thing that fits in the car-seat base. Or the buggy."

Kade's gaze settled on a box on the floor. Snagging it, he slit the tape holding it closed and pulled out something that resembled a small backpack. "You can use this, too. We have one like it. You stick the baby in it and strap it on, carrying her across your chest. As long as it's not subfreezing, you could at least go feed the horses." Kade and his new wife were expecting, and apparently he'd done his homework. He looked down at the toes of his boots. "You do know you can't put her in the car seat in the truck and just…leave her, right?"

Deke didn't laugh, but he wanted to. "Yeah. Got that. She needs to be right there within sight because…helpless baby." He didn't add the "duh" but it was implied.

Laughing softly, Kade nodded. "Yeah, figured. But you know, the women…" They exchanged knowing looks. "Have you thought about hiring a nanny or something?"

"Cash will find the mom before long. I can cope until then. Or call the Bee Dubyas in a pinch."

Kade laughed again. "That's true. Anyway, if you need me, I can come feed, or I can send one of my hands."

"Dude, you're going to have your own hands full soon enough. Pippa looks like she's ready to pop any day now."

Kade blanched and sank onto the end of the bed. "Yeah." He looked up, his expression bleak. "I'm terrified."

Gazing down at the baby now sleeping so peacefully in his arms, Deke murmured, "Yeah, I know the feeling."

Quin would have banged her head against the steering wheel but she was driving at highway speeds on the interstate.

Her visit with Deacon couldn't have gone any worse. As soon as she saw all the vehicles in the drive, she should have turned around and…what? Run away like a scared dog with her tail tucked between legs? She *really* needed to find the mother, like yesterday!

Determined to do just that, she headed toward Troop A HQ, rather than home. She had a change of civilian clothes in her locker there. It was Sunday. The place would be quiet and she'd have access to databases from the department computer that she wouldn't have on her laptop at home.

Eight hours later, her stomach burned from too much caffeine and too little food. She had a list of people to contact on Monday, when state offices were open. Leaning back in her squeaky desk chair, she closed her eyes and swiveled a little from side to side. She tapped out a rhythm on her desk with a pen. What if Noelle's mother wasn't a native Oklahoman? If she was simply a fan of Deacon's, the girl could have come from any of the surrounding states.

Sitting up with a sigh, she made more notes: Arkansas, Missouri, Kansas, Texas. Midwives. Hospitals. She doodled on her pad, realized the black lines vaguely resembled a bus. How had she gotten to Thunder River? She added cab companies to her list. And bus lines. If the girl came in from out of state, maybe she got here by bus. With luck, they'd still have security footage at the station downtown.

Quin dropped her chin to her chest and rubbed her stiff neck muscles. She had no idea when the girl had arrived. It would take days to go through the footage and all she had to go on was a woman carrying a baby in a basket. *Needle, meet haystack.* Pushing back from the desk, she walked to the window, to discover that night had fallen. Time for a hot shower and a good night's sleep, then she'd hit the investigation hard in the morning, which was Monday. Ugh.

A half hour later, after a stop for fast food, she stood under the steaming spray of water in her shower. Tension melted from her body, and her mind drifted to the one place she really needed to avoid—thoughts of Deacon Tate. And that kiss. The feel of his body—far more muscular than she would have guessed—pressed against hers. With the weight and stiffness of her Kevlar vest between them.

She'd spent a lot of time observing the man. The way his long hair fell across his forehead. His dreamy blue eyes that could go from star sapphire to ice at the whim of his mood. Broad shoulders. Muscular arms and chest. Lean hips. And his hands. Yes, she pretty much had a love affair going with his hands. He had long fingers and the strength in them was evident every time he touched her. She knew his fingertips were calloused and rough from when he'd touched her bare skin.

And she was right back to their kiss. His kiss. He'd kissed her. She hadn't kissed him back. Nope. Not. At. All. Quin thunked her forehead against the tile. That kiss could never repeat itself. It had been a huge breach of ethics. Not to mention that Deacon Tate could be dangerous to her equilibrium. And her heart.

Sleep was out of the question now. Her body was hot and achy. She slid her hands over her torso and stomach and pretended he was touching her. She replayed the kiss in her memory, the way his teeth nipped her lips, the way his tongue teased against hers. Quin could almost taste the way his skin had smelled—tart lemon and almondlike cookies, sage and cedar like walking in the woods.

So much for a hot shower. If she was smart, she'd switch the knob to Cold. Since she wasn't much of a masochist, she left the water temperature alone and just gave in to the urges created by thoughts of the sexy singer. She wasn't sure how much longer she could resist his charms.

Her visits needed to be perfunctory—a quick peek at the kid and then she'd hit the road. No problem. The less time she spent with Mr. Too Sexy For His Jeans, the better. And she needed leads to find the baby momma, who was the basis of this whole fiasco. The water went lukewarm and she shut it off. Nothing like a good dose of thinking about work to get her back on track.

Quin always volunteered to work Thanksgiving Day. Other troopers had families to share the day with and the last place she wanted to be was with hers. She'd rather be out on the highways making sure other families got safely to their destinations. Except this Thanksgiving, she had one extra duty. *Ugh.*

Not knowing how Deacon planned to spend the day, she'd called ahead…only to learn he was at his mother's place. With the whole family. Tates *and* Barrons. *Double ugh.*

She had a plan. She would duck in, make sure the

baby was happy and whole, and run. Because the last thing she wanted, after last Saturday and Sunday, was to be trapped in a house with all those people.

A Mercedes blew past her. She automatically hit her lights and siren and charged after the speeder. Quin called in the vehicle description and license plate. The car came back clear, meaning it wasn't reported stolen and the tag was up-to-date. Five miles later, the driver realized she was chasing behind. He pulled to the shoulder and the brake lights went off. Good. The driver had put the sedan in Park.

Still, she approached cautiously. Like domestics, seemingly normal traffic stops could go south in a hurry. "Please turn off the ignition," she called, easing up to the side of the car, one hand on the roof, the other on her pistol. The driver immediately complied. Quin leaned down to look in the window.

A very sheepish man with gray hair and Clark Kent glasses offered an apologetic smile. "I am so sorry, officer. I fear I wasn't paying attention."

She didn't acknowledge the apology. "License, registration and proof of insurance, please."

The guy patted his jacket, doing his best to look bemused. Quin's instincts kicked in. "Please step out of the car, sir."

She backed up to give him room. A second later, she had a fight on her hands. The guy erupted from the driver's seat, fists swinging. She ducked the first punch but the follow-through caught her on the cheek and it *hurt*. Still the man was out of shape and she wasn't.

Quin had him subdued within a few short minutes, but she'd taken a few more licks in the process.

"What is your problem, mister?" she asked as backup arrived and hoisted the man to his feet.

"Do you know who I am?"

Quin closed her eyes, counted to ten and took a deep breath. "No. Because you decided to turn stupid before you handed me your driver's license." The man opened his mouth to tell her and she held up a hand. "Too late now and I don't really care what your name is. You assaulted a state trooper. You are going to jail."

About to lose her cool again, she backed away and let the other officers deal with him. In short order, the driver was identified, Mirandized and stuffed in the back seat of another trooper's cruiser. "You really should hit the ER, Quin," one of the officers said.

"Yeah, yeah. It's just a bruise and a split lip. There's another deal I have to take care of first. I'll stop by University Hospital on my way home just for the paperwork. My LT is gonna be really unhappy. He was off today."

After a bit of commiseration from the other troopers who had responded, Quin was back in her cruiser driving to the last place in the world she wanted to be. After dealing with this ego-inflated, entitled jerk, she was headed into a nest of more just like him.

The celebration wasn't quite in full swing yet. Deke was hanging out close to the front door. Not *hovering* exactly, but he wanted to be the one to answer when Quin arrived.

The place was crawling with Tates and Barrons. As far as his mother was concerned, the more, the merrier. She and his late uncle Cyrus were as opposite as two siblings could get, except for one thing: when it came to family loyalty, they'd been peas in a pod.

The sun was shining, the air chilly but comfortable and there would be football after lunch, but not on TV. Any shared holiday—Thanksgiving, Christmas, Easter, Fourth of July, it didn't matter—always ended in a game of pickup football between the Tates and the Barrons. This year, the game would be a little less cutthroat given that little CJ would be playing.

When the doorbell rang, Deke just managed to beat Dillon to it. They scuffled and Deke had his little brother in a headlock when the door opened. Quin stood there, her uniform rumpled, a dark bruise on her cheek threatening to spread to her eye, her lip cut and swollen.

"What the hell—" He pushed Dillon away and reached for Quin's arm, drawing her into the room. "Who hit you?" Anger sat like a frozen lump of cornbread dressing in his gut.

Dillon, standing beside him, sucked in air. "Dang, Deke."

"I'm fine," Quin insisted, looking distinctly uncomfortable. "I just had a small run-in with a speeder. Not a big deal."

"The hell you say." Deke normally didn't cuss. Katherine Tate had certain rules in her house and four-letter words were prohibited. At the moment, he really didn't care. "If you could see your face, Quin, you'd say different."

His mother was suddenly at his other side, having pushed through the mass of people who'd rushed the door after hearing Deke's raised voice. "Let the child in," she insisted.

"I'm not a child," Quin said.

"In my house, if you're hurt, you're a child. And you're bleeding."

"But I'm not—"

Deke brushed his index finger over her chin and held it up for her to see the bloodstained tip. "Yeah, darlin', you are. Come in."

"Come with me," his mom ordered.

She and Quin, followed closely by Jolie, disappeared into the interior of the house. All the rest of the family stood around in stunned silence until CJ piped up. "She had a bad boo-boo, Cuncle Deke. You shoulda kissed it. That's what Mommy and Daddy do for me."

Cuncle was a word CJ had coined to differentiate between his Barron uncles and his corresponding Tate cousins. Normally, Deke would have smiled at the kid but he was way too angry. Cord, CJ's dad, shushed him and suggested that they go see what was on TV.

Deke had to find out exactly what had happened and if Quin really was okay. He arrived at the door to the bathroom, standing just out of sight.

"Yes, Mrs. Tate. I fully intend on going to the ER. It's required by DPS."

His mother immediately scolded Quin. "You shouldn't be driving, young lady."

"Mrs. Barron—" Quin began.

"Call me Jolie."

"Will you please explain to her that I'm fine?" Quin sounded exasperated and frustrated.

Deke settled on a plan. He'd have to make arrangements for Noelle but he would insist on driving Quin to the ER. She still had a chip on her shoulder where he and his family were concerned and he had a major hankering to knock off that chip. To take care of her. Not to mention kiss her. Again.

Deke slipped out before he got caught eavesdropping and was sitting on a bar stool jostling Noelle on his knee when the three women returned. As he'd anticipated, his mother insisted Quin join them for lunch though it took the threat of calling her supervisor to get her to sit down and eat.

The Barrons and their wives gathered on one side of the massive farm table. The Tates lined the other. Deke's mom sat at one end and his oldest brother, Hunter, who served as chief of security for Clay Barron, sat at the other. Deke did his best to steer Quin away from Dillon, but his irritating little brother grabbed the chair next to her when Tucker distracted Deke.

Taking matters into his own hands, Deke pulled out the empty chair on Quin's other side, picked up her chair—with her sitting in it—and set it down in the empty spot. Then he hooked the empty chair with his booted foot, dragged it into place and sat. He smirked at Dillon before turning a sunny smile on Quin. She was working her lips to hide her smile.

"Don't you have brothers?" he asked, acting all innocent.

"I do. Four of them."

"Then you should be used to stupid antics."

She raised an eyebrow over her uninjured eye and didn't bother to hide her own smirk. "You could say that."

"So," Dillon said, leaning around Deke, "did you get the license of the truck that hit you?" He *oofed* as Deke nailed him in the ribs with an elbow.

Their mother cleared her throat and gave Dillon and him her "mother stare." Then she smiled at Quin. "I suppose your brothers taught you lots of things growing up."

"Yes, ma'am, they did."

Dillon leaned over Deke again, still grinning. "Oh? Care to share?"

She fixed Dillon with a regal expression that was almost as good as his mom's. "They taught me what not to date."

Nine

Deke, taking a sip of water at the time, spluttered and coughed. Dillon was all too happy to pound on his back. When he could breathe again, his mom fixed him with a stare. "I like this one."

Great. His mother had never been subtle and the few women he'd brought to family gatherings had never measured up to Katherine Tate's strict standards for her boys. Now she put her seal of approval on a maddening cop who made him think very inappropriate thoughts about her and handcuffs. He managed to avoid looks from both women by keeping his head down and stuffing the traditional Thanksgiving meal into his mouth.

By the time lunch was over, Quin's shiner was a doozy and her eye was swollen almost shut. He exchanged a look with his mother over pumpkin pie. He was formally excused from clean-up duty. His mother was as concerned about Quin's injuries as he was and would back him up when he insisted on driving her into Oklahoma City to University Hospital to get checked out.

The argument was brief when he told Quin the plan. He paused to grab an ice pack from the freezer before gathering her up and ushering her toward the door. His brothers were teaching CJ to do whipped-cream shots straight from the can as he closed the door behind them.

Deke guided her to his truck, and she balked until he said, "Do you want me to drive your cruiser? Because, babe, I've always wanted to go code three."

"What about the baby?"

Laughter rumbled in his throat and he didn't even attempt to stop it. "Darlin', my mother has seven sons. Not one of us is married, nor do we have any kids. She's in hog heaven babysittin' that little girl. Not to mention the Bee Dubyas."

"Bee what-yas?"

He spelled out the words as he settled her into the passenger seat of his truck and buckled the seat belt before she could. Then he explained, "Bee Dubya. For Barron Wives. That's what we call them when they're runnin' in a posse like they sometimes do."

He handed Quin the ice pack and she gingerly pressed it against her cheek. Deke didn't miss the wince and found himself doing the same in sympathy.

Neither of them spoke on the drive to the hospital. Walking in with an injured Highway Patrol trooper was a fast way to get in and out of the ER. Her X-rays were negative. The lip was already scabbing over. Thanks to the ice pack on the trip into town, the swelling around Quin's eye was down but she had a heck of a shiner. The ER doc wanted her to go home to bed. Deke perked up at that instruction and grinned when Quin scowled.

She was hurt. A tender part of him that didn't often see the light of day just wanted to offer comfort. The tenderness he felt toward this feisty woman should have made him nervous. He wanted to ascribe the feeling to being around the baby, but he had been contemplating a home and family before any of this happened. Bottom line? He was all kinds of interested in Quincy.

They ended up compromising, not that he was happy about it. He drove her back to his mom's, then strapped Noelle, snugly asleep in her carrier, into the base of the car seat in his truck, and followed Quin, who was driving her cruiser, home. "Just in case," he'd insisted. Of course, he hadn't mentioned his ulterior motives— like finding out where she lived. The strain of the fight was settling in and her muscles were most likely stiff. She couldn't take any of the super-duper pain pills the doctor prescribed until she was safely home.

Deke was right on her bumper as she keyed in through the gate of her complex and he slipped through on her tail. His mom would have his head if he didn't see Quin safely to her door. That explanation was on the tip of his tongue as she confronted him when he pulled up behind her cruiser.

He rolled down the back window so he could hear the baby if she stirred and stepped out of the pickup, hands up in surrender. "Don't care what you say, dar-lin'."

"Stop calling me that."

"Okay, Trooper Darlin'. Whatever you say. But I'm tellin' ya, my momma would have my head if she heard I'd just left you here and driven away. I'll sit here until you're safely inside."

She angled her head, and he could almost see the thoughts tumbling behind her calculating gaze. "You aren't going to insist on coming in?"

Deke gestured to the open window of his truck. "Little bit is sleepin'. I'm not gonna wake her, and I sure don't plan on leavin' her alone in the truck."

He reached out and gently traced the tip of a finger along the uninjured side of her jaw. "The man who did this deserves to spend a long time in jail," he said, his voice quiet but threatening. She tensed at his words but he leaned in anyway and planted a soft kiss on the corner of her mouth. "Go get some sleep, darlin'. I'll see ya soon."

He gripped her shoulders, turned her around and gave her a nudge toward her condo. Deke waited until she'd unlocked the door before he climbed back into the truck. He didn't stop the grin when he saw her raise her hand and touch the corner of her mouth where he'd kissed her. Yeah…he planned on seeing a lot more of Trooper Kincaid.

The day after Thanksgiving, Quin awoke stiff and achy, and the thought of getting out of bed filled her with dread. She poked at her bottom lip and winced.

"Not too bright, dummy," she chided herself. Her lip was still swollen, as was that whole side of her face.

Quin brushed the tip of her index finger over the spot where Deacon's lips had brushed her mouth last night. She hadn't expected the kiss—or maybe she had, but not the sweetness of it, or the tenderness of his touch.

How could she be so stupid? There was no way she was getting involved with Deacon. No. Just no. It was all kinds of wrong on more levels than she could comprehend this morning. First, he was part of a case she was working on. Second, he was bad news and she didn't trust him. She needed the DNA proof from the paternity test. The results were slowed down by the holiday but she held out hope they'd arrive within the next couple of weeks. Discovering whether he was the father would answer a lot of her questions.

Did they have chemistry? Well, she was human. And female. And he was Deacon Tate. His fame put her off more than it attracted her, but she had to admit, he was sexier than all get-out when he was up on stage singing. She made a mental note to never use her computer at Troop A to watch his YouTube videos again.

So she was attracted to him. No big deal since she had no intention of ever stepping over the professional line again. And so what if he flirted with her. He was a man who lived for the adoration of his female fans. Obviously. He was charming. Handsome. Talented. Sexy.

Quin groaned. This line of thought was taking her nowhere. She rolled out of bed with as few movements as possible. A long, hot shower would ease some of the pain and would definitely help with the stiffness. Then she'd check in at Troop A to see if any new information about Noelle's mother had arrived. She was tugging on every string she had looking for a lead. Then she'd face the drive to Deacon's ranch.

An hour later, she walked into the briefing at Troop A to the sound of whistles and catcalls. She kept her cop face in place, ignoring them as she took a seat. Staff meetings only happened once a week. The rest of the time, troopers checked in with Dispatch and hit the highway—or other assigned duties—running. Just her luck, the briefing had been scheduled for today.

The lieutenant walked to the podium, stared around the room making a head count, then launched into the game plan for the holiday weekend. It seemed everyone but Quin would be back out on the highways for the travel rush. It rankled that the lieutenant singled her out to come to his office as they broke up.

As soon as he closed his office door behind her, she opened her mouth to complain but he interrupted with a brusque "How's the face?"

"Sore."

"I want you to go home." He shook his head at her. "No arguments. You still need to check on the kid, then you can work from home, where you'll be comfortable. You can follow up leads from there."

If she had any. Still, the idea of a long, hot bath, flannel pajamas and fuzzy slippers appealed.

"Rest up because I need you back on patrol duty tomorrow. And trust me, I'd be saying this to any trooper whose face looked like yours. You can arrange your check on Deacon Tate around the patrol schedule. Okay?" He flashed her a droll smile. "I know you've been chewing your leash, Kincaid. Get over it. You're very much in the public eye. We need to find the mother then turn this whole mess over to those with more political clout than we have."

"No kidding, sir."

"Then get to work."

"Sir, yes, sir."

When her cruiser rolled to a stop in front of Deacon's house, there were no other vehicles around. Weird. Every other time she'd been here, the place had seemed like traffic central. Did he have a garage? She got out and looked around. No movement anywhere. She strode up the walk and climbed the steps to the front porch. Still nothing. She knocked, then walked around the house peeking in windows. No movement. No sound.

Her emotions seesawed between worry and anger. On her second circuit of the house, movement down at one of the outbuildings caught her eye. She went back to her cruiser and drove to what turned out to be the barn. A man she'd never seen before was in the process of releasing several horses into a corral.

"Can I help ya?" the man called.

"I'm looking for Mr. Tate."

The man pushed his ball cap up and scratched at the thatch of hair that spilled across his forehead. "Well now, I probably need t'know why you're lookin' for the boss."

Quin approached the fence. "And you are?"

He walked over and stuck out his hand. "Matt McConaughey." He patted his ample middle and laughed at her skeptical expression. "I know. I get that reaction a lot. I manage the place for Deke when he's outta town. Now, why would an Oklahoma Highway Patrol trooper be lookin' for my boss?"

"The same reason I've been out here every day for the past week. He has a baby—"

"Oh, yeah. I heard about that." He pointed toward a house off in the distance. "I live over there. Don't pay much attention to the comings and goings at the big house."

"Well, I've been assigned to make a daily welfare check on the baby. I need to know where Mr. Tate is and, more importantly, where the baby is."

"Don't gotta clue 'bout the baby. Deke headed to Tulsa early this mornin'. The boys gotta concert there t'night."

A concert? In Tulsa? Where was the baby? Angry, she took out her phone and called the number she had for Deke. It went straight to voice mail. Why hadn't he told her he was leaving town? He knew she made this ridiculous trip every day. And was he stupid enough to drag the baby to a freaking concert?

Realizing she'd hung up before leaving a message, she called back. This time she left an earful. She ignored the grinning cowboy watching her. After ending the call, she didn't even try to mask her irritation, though she remained civil to the man. "I appreciate your help."

"I'm sure I'll see ya again, Trooper Kincaid. Drive safe now."

When she got to the ranch gate, Quin stopped the cruiser but let it idle. She would have to drive to Tulsa now. Except she had no idea where the blasted concert was taking place. She grabbed her cell and did a search. The Sons of Nashville were scheduled to play at the BOK Center, starting at 7:00 p.m. So why the heck were they already up there?

So much for a hot bath, flannel and fuzzies. No way would she task a Troop B officer with tracking down the errant singer. Nope. Quin wanted to tell him what she thought of him in person.

Two and a half hours later, she pulled up in front of the tour bus and parked. She was about to use her baton on the door when it swooshed open and a smiling Max Padilla greeted her.

"Well, howdy, Miss, er, Trooper Kincaid. I wasn't expectin' t'see you."

Quin stifled the irritation that had simmered into anger on the drive. It wasn't this man's fault that his boss was a major pain in her butt. "I'm here to see Mr. Tate."

He offered a grin and a little wink, which just added to her irritation. "I'm guessin' that would be Mr. Deke and not Mr. Dillon."

"That would be a good guess."

"He's inside the BOK, ma'am."

She didn't trust her voice so she dipped her chin in a clipped nod to acknowledge the information. Her body cringed with each stomping step she took to the backstage entrance and she hoped she had some ibuprofen in the cruiser. She pressed the button on the keypad and identified herself when security answered. It still took her another ten minutes to get to the room set aside for the band.

Listening at the door before knocking, Quin caught feminine laughter fluttering above the more guttural sounds from the men. If someone asked, she would have been hard-pressed to explain the emotions roiling inside her and she would never utter out loud the names she was calling Deacon.

She banged on the door and waited. Someone called, "It's open. C'mon in."

As Quin pressed down on the lever, she heard someone else say, "I hope that's catering. I'm starved."

Opening the door wide, she stepped into the room. Silence descended with the force of a thunderclap. A couple of guys wearing tour T-shirts exchanged nervous glances. One of the girls tittered. Another retained her seat in the lap of one of the band members and watched with an amused expression on her face. Scanning faces, Quin located Deacon sitting in the rear of the room, removed from everyone else.

"Well, well, well," he drawled. "Fancy meeting you here, Trooper Kincaid."

"We need to talk."

"Okay."

She stared around the room to make the point that she wanted the conversation to be private. He just grinned at her, that darn brow quirked in a mischievous arch. Great. She could ignore his appeal and if he didn't mind an audience, who was she to argue?

"Why didn't you tell me you'd be out of town?"

"Didn't know I needed to. Besides, it isn't much of a secret, darlin'. Every country station in the state has been advertising this concert."

"You could have told me." Okay, now she just sounded whiny. She inhaled deeply and blew out the breath to calm down. "You are aware that part of my duty as the lead officer on the baby Noelle case includes a daily welfare check."

"Is that why you've been comin' by the ranch?" He winked at her. "I thought you were comin' to see me."

"As if." When Deacon laughed, she realized she'd muttered that loud enough for him to hear. "Where's Noelle?" She put every bit of haughty authority she was still clinging to into her tone.

"She's in Oklahoma City."

"Well, at least you didn't drag a baby all the way up here and subject her to—to…" Words failed and Quin resorted to waving her hands around the room. That's when she realized every person there was watching, fascinated by her exchange with Deacon. "What did you do? Call up one of your groupies to babysit? You can't be doing things like this, Mr. Tate. You have a responsibility to that child. One, I'll remind you, that you agreed…no, you *insisted* on accepting. You can't just drop a baby off willy-nilly."

He mouthed *willy-nilly* and curled his lips between his teeth in what appeared to be an effort not to laugh.

"I'm serious, Mr. Tate. I would think you'd have more sense than to leave that child with just anyone."

Deacon's expression morphed from one of playfulness to one tinged with irritation. "Ah. So you're accusing me of being so callous that I'd dump the little girl I'd agreed to take care of on just *anyone*?"

There was a trap here but Quin was tired, annoyed and in pain. She couldn't see it so rather than saying a word, she nodded.

"You mean just *anyone*…like my mother."

Ten

His mother. Of course. What was she thinking? Oh, wait, she hadn't been thinking.

The scene kept playing over and over in her memory as she drove back to Oklahoma City. There'd been no humor in his expression when he'd told her where Noelle was. Feeling like an idiot—as she should—Quin had stood there with her mouth all but gaping as the implications hit her. No one in that room had said a word and she could relate to how a deflated balloon felt. Exiting with as much grace as she could muster, she'd all but run to her cruiser.

And here she was, headed southwest toward Oklahoma City. Quin glanced at the speedometer. A steady seventy-five—the speed limit. She had a lead foot but she was tempted to ease off. Her speed dropped five miles per hour. She was in no hurry to see Mrs. Tate because she had every reason to believe that as soon as she left the green room at the BOK, Deacon had called his mother.

What could she say to the woman? Worse, what would the woman say to her? Quin knew from the moment she'd first laid eyes on Katherine Tate that the matriarch would fight like a momma bear for her boys. Watching their interaction at breakfast that first morning, she'd figured Deacon was very likely a favorite son.

The closer she got to Oklahoma City, the slower she drove. Quin stretched out the drive as long as she could. Once she hit the city limits, though, she had no more excuses. She'd already notified Dispatch of her destination and received directions instead of an address. Having met the woman, Quin was surprised not to be headed to Nichols Hills or one of the other wealthy enclaves. Nope. Just like her son, she lived out in the country on the family ranch. Why couldn't these people live in the city like normal folks?

Quin pulled through the ranch gate and slowly drove up the gravel drive. As she passed, cows happily munching the winter-brown grass lifted their heads to watch. Who had cows in their front yard? A man on horseback rode toward the cows and waved at her. Okay, maybe they were cattle instead of cows. There was a difference. The road took a gentle curve through an alley of trees, their bare branches entwining overhead.

When she saw the house, she stopped her cruiser.

It was nothing like what she expected. It was huge and sprawling, and if she'd driven up here on a dark, stormy night, she probably would have turned around and high-tailed it out of there. She'd read too many Gothic novels as a kid. The home positively loomed from the top of a hill. It had three stories, a gabled roof, columns and was covered in what the locals called giraffe stone. Two one-story wings stretched from each end. The porch ran the length of the main portion of the house, its white columns supporting a balcony accessible from the second floor.

Quin sighed deeply and squared her shoulders. The sooner she could see the baby and run, the better. But when she parked she didn't get out of the car because she still had no idea what to say to Mrs. Tate.

The front doors opened and a tall woman in jeans, boots and a chambray shirt stepped out onto the porch. She jammed her hands on her hips and hollered, "You gonna sit out there all day, Trooper Kincaid, or are you gonna come inside and be civilized?"

There was no hope now. Infused with dread, Quin got out and approached. Her booted feet clomped on the steps, their cadence giving away her reluctance.

"Don't dawdle, girl. I got things to do before the sun goes down."

She quickened her pace and Quin looked up to meet Mrs. Tate's sharp gaze. She'd thought the woman was wearing a work shirt. She'd been wrong. The blouse was a chambray blue but carried the sheen of polished cotton. It had a scene of snow-covered evergreens and cardinals delicately embroidered across the front. Quin caught the soft off-white gleam of pearls at the open collar. Her gaze flicked up just in time to catch a fleeting smile on Mrs. Tate's face.

What was it about this woman and pearls?

"Mom will deal with her."

Deacon glanced up at his youngest brother. He expected to see a mischievous expression to match Dillon's teasing tone. He found sympathy instead. He nodded in agreement but said nothing.

"I wouldn't wanna be that trooper by the time Mom's done with her."

He shrugged absently, plucking a tune from his guitar.

"Look, Deke, I know y'all think I'm young and stuff but I'm not as clueless as I act."

"I know that." He strummed through a chord progression. "What are you after, little bro?"

"Nothin'. I just figure you might want someone to talk to. I mean, dude! You're a single dad. Out of the blue. How crazy is that?" Dillon dropped onto the couch beside him. "Are you worried about the test results? What if she's yours?"

"She's not mine, Dill Pickle." Deke reverted to his brother's childhood nickname in hopes the other man would go away.

"Then why are you fighting to keep her?"

"I'm not. Not exactly."

Dillon pushed the sunglasses propped on the top of his head down to cover his eyes. Then he dramatically pulled them down his nose and leaned forward, peering intently over those glasses. "Seriously?"

His brother's antics made him laugh, which Deke suspected had been Dillon's intent all along. "Fine. Busted. I don't think she's mine, though we need the DNA part of the paternity test anyway. Chance says women are coming out of the woodwork to claim Noelle. The police kept the contents of the note out of the news, and it hasn't leaked so far. That's one way we can determine a legitimate claim. The other will be a confirmation of mitochondrial DNA from the mother."

"Woo, listen to you, Mr. Smart Guy. Maybe those college classes stuck after all."

"Or I watch too many reality-based crime shows when I can't sleep."

They both laughed. Deke welcomed the companionship. But after a moment, Dillon continued his interrogation. "You know I'm gonna ask. Everyone is wondering but Mom told us to stay out of it."

With a long-suffering sigh, Deke said, "Go ahead. Get it off your chest."

"Why?"

Deacon played a few more chords, paused to make notations in a musical composition notebook, strummed again. "Christmas is coming up. I have the feeling the mother will come back for Noelle. If the baby is in the system, she might never get her back."

"Uh-huh." The disbelief in Dillon's voice earned him a look.

"Uh-huh, Dill. If it turns out she's capable of taking care of the baby, I'll help her get Noelle back."

"Why would you help her?"

He lifted a shoulder and continued composing the tune. "How desperate do you have to be to drop your baby off at a band's tour bus? I'm bettin' the mom's not much more than a kid herself. She saw the bus, got this harebrained idea and boom. I have a baby. If the mom is honest with me, and she's not strung out or something, I'll do what I can for her."

Dillon snatched the notebook and made his own notations before pushing it back. "Play it that way."

Deke did and smiled. "Much better. Thanks."

"You're welcome." Dillon listened to him play some more, then asked, "Now tell me the real reason."

That was the question of the day, wasn't it? Deke had been mulling over reasons since he'd first laid eyes on the angelic child. "I wish I knew. I took one look and fell in love with her. It's hard—taking care of Noelle. Lord knows I'm exhausted all the time. I lay awake at night listening to her breathe and start freaking out about SIDS or croup. Colic. She'll be teething before too long."

"Uh-huh."

Deke hummed a vocal line over the chords he was strumming, both stalling and gathering his thoughts. "It's crazy, Dillon, but I want a family. I look at the Barron boys. I watch Cord with CJ. I see the others with their Bee Dubyas. They're happy. They want to go home at night. With Noelle around, I don't want to *leave* home. I want to adopt her if the mother doesn't turn up. I want to find a woman I love so much that I want to make our own babies because I want Noelle to have brothers and sisters. I want to fill my house as full as our house was growing up."

Reaching over to feel Deke's forehead and laughing when his brother slapped his hand away, Dillon said, "Nope. No fever. You do realize that finding a woman who wants seven kids in this day and age is like finding a…" He flapped his hands in the air like he was searching for inspiration. "That kind of woman is so rare there's nothing to compare it to."

"I don't have eight bedrooms and dang if I'll make my kids share a bedroom. You had it easy, kid. Hunter was already out of the house, plus Mom and Dad had added on their master suite so you got your own room. I had to share a room with Tucker. And he snored like a diesel truck when he was two. I just want Noelle to have some siblings. When a kid's an only child, it makes me kinda sad."

"Uh-huh." Dillon leaned away but he wasn't quite fast enough. Deacon's fist tagged him on the biceps with a teasing punch. "All right, all right," he laughed. "So, do you have someone in mind?" He waggled his brows suggestively.

"No."

"Yeah, right. You answered my question way too fast, Deke. I'm thinkin' you've taken a fancy to the trooper."

"No!" Okay. Maybe he shouldn't have been quite so forceful with that denial because Dillon was now having trouble breathing around the laughter. "She's not interested in me or kids, Dill. You've seen her. She goes white every time someone even looks like they might hand her the baby."

"Mom likes her," Dillon wheezed.

"Shut. Up."

Dillon laughed harder. When he could breathe, he huffed out, "You *are* interested in her. Gotta say she certainly—"

"Don't go there, Dillon. I'm warning you." Deke was all but growling. His little brother was saved by a knock on the door.

"Yo, dudes!" Kenji stuck his head in. "We're on in, like, five."

Quin perched on the edge of a leather couch. A silver serving tray with a complete silver coffee-and-tea service reigned over a slate coffee table. Who still entertained a guest like this? Oh, yeah, a woman who wore pearls with her jeans and cowboy boots. She placed Mrs. Tate in her early sixties but this setup was a throwback to the *Leave It to Beaver* days of the fifties.

Mrs. Tate had convinced her to stay for dinner. Okay, she wouldn't take no for an answer. Quin had even been forced to hold the baby for a bit—just so she could ascertain for herself that Noelle was fine and well cared for, as Mrs. Tate explained. The dig in that comment was apparent and Quincy had blushed. Now, what seemed like hours later, here they were having tea and coffee.

Mrs. Tate sat regally, spine straight, shoulders square, chin up—her posture perfect. Quin had no trouble picturing this woman looking right at home in *Downton Abbey*. "I do appreciate you staying for a visit, Quincy. We're still friends so I can call you Quincy, right?"

"Of c-course." Darn it. Why did she have to stammer? Quincy steadied the china cup and saucer holding her coffee on her knee.

"Please call me Katherine. I suspect we might become better friends before all is said and done."

Katherine smiled at her and while it looked benign enough, Quin saw the shark swimming behind the woman's expression. Quin was skating on thin ice and she knew it. She nodded and offered a partial smile but kept her mouth shut.

"Since you have such a large place in my son's life, Quincy, I thought it wise for us to get to know one another."

"No, ma'am." At the woman's raised brow, Quin scrambled to explain. "What I mean, ma'am, is that I have no place in Deacon's life. I'm here only to deal with the baby during the course of my investigation. Once the mother is located and a determination is made about the best interest of the child, then I'm…"

"You're what, Quincy?"

"No longer involved."

"Are you involved?" That shark smile again. "With my son?"

"Good heavens, no!" Quin wanted to bite her tongue. Time to backpedal. "What I mean is, your son… I… There's… No. Just…no. We aren't involved. Not like you're insinuating. And we won't be. I'm a state trooper doing my job. Your… Deacon… He's…"

"Handsome?" Now Katherine's smile was cat-and-cream smug. "Talented?"

"Ah, well, yes. Of course he is. But he and I… We aren't…"

"Did you know my mother was a good Southern woman?"

Quincy's head spun from the lightning-fast change in subject. "I… No. I know nothing about your family."

Now Katherine's smile was indulgent. "But you should, dear. Momma came from Georgia. She met Daddy at a cotillion in Atlanta. He was this brash westerner come east to get gentrified because he'd already made his first million. He was a rancher and an oilman. Tall and handsome, and Momma said it was love at first sight. They eloped, much to her parents' consternation. At least until they got a gander at Daddy's bank account. That made him their favorite son-in-law."

The older woman's right hand went to her throat, her fingers lovingly stroking the pearl necklace framed by the collar and open placket of her blouse. "Momma always wore pearls, you see." She sat up straighter—if that was even possible—and her voice took on a deep Southern drawl. "She used to say 'A Southern woman always has a string of pearls, Katherine. They give her grace and beauty even when she's feeling clumsy and ugly. They give her something to clutch when she wants to wring her hands.'" Katherine added, in her own voice, "One must never wring one's hands, no matter how dire the situation, you see." She tilted her head as if listening to something outside and smiled.

Quincy heard it then…the soft whump-whump-

whump of a helicopter. Wait? The Tates had a helicopter pad? *And* a helicopter? Who in the world was arriv— Deacon. Of course. Moments later, she watched through the wide windows of the living room as the helicopter landed, its door opened and Deacon ducked out. Before she could catch her breath, Deacon was striding into the room. He stopped to kiss his mother's cheek, then asked, "Where's my girl?"

"Upstairs, son, but she's sleepin'. Don't go botherin' her now. Girls need their beauty sleep."

He laughed and leaped up the stairs two at a time. "Just gotta make sure she's sleepin' sweet."

As soon as Deacon was out of sight, Quincy gulped down her lukewarm coffee and wondered how to extricate herself. He wouldn't be gone more than a couple of minutes and she had no clue how to avoid seeing him when he returned. Her instincts told her to just get up and run.

Katherine leaned over and patted her knee. "You really should think about getting some pearls, Quincy."

Eleven

Deacon had been doing his best to sleep in. Noelle had suffered a touch of colic and after a slightly panicked middle-of-the-night call to Jolie—because there was no way he was getting his mother involved—he'd loaded the baby into his truck and they'd gone on a road trip around the countryside until Noelle fell asleep. He discovered she preferred love ballads like Dierks Bentley's "Black" and Jason Aldean's "Burnin' It Down." Too bad those songs sent his thoughts rocketing straight back to the kiss with Quin that should never have happened. Though now that it had, Deke was more than ready to seduce Trooper Kincaid into his bed, bad idea though it might be. She didn't like him, didn't trust him. Maybe it was the idea of forbidden fruit...

He shook the thought out of his head. Any pursuit

of the lovely trooper was a bad idea. Not to mention his mother liked her. That fact should have him running away as fast as he could go. Remembering his discussion with Dillon, he reminded himself that he and Noelle were just a job to Quin, that she didn't have a motherly bone in her body. Sure she was sexy, but she wasn't forever.

Half-awake, he continued contemplating the events of the past several weeks. Ignoring the prickle in the back of his mind about the test results being due any time, Deke thought about the sexy trooper. He was a perverse son of a gun for enjoying his daily visits with Quin, not to mention that he was totally smitten with the baby girl asleep down the hall. Needling the trooper to get a reaction out of her was becoming a favorite pastime.

He drifted into a light doze, the sexy cop filling his mind.

Pounding on the door roused him from a vivid dream about the trooper and her handcuffs. Huh, who knew? That kink was becoming more interesting. Wearing only sleep pants slung low on his hips, he stumbled to the front door. To avoid waking up to a horde of relatives, he'd reprogrammed the electronic unlock code. Punching in the new sequence, he expected to find his mother or one of the Bee Dubyas when he opened the door.

Instead, he got the very woman of his dream. He caught her with her hand raised, ready to knock again. Her eyes widened as her gaze trailed from his face, down across his chest—and lower. Already aroused, his body reacted even more. Did Quin's pupils dilate? Her nostrils definitely flared and yeah, there was pink in her cheeks probably not brought on by the chilly temperature.

"You're early." Deke yawned and scrubbed his fingers through his messy hair.

"Obviously."

"Come in. I'll make some coffee." He stepped back so she could walk through the door.

Deke remembered to shut the door as Quin slipped past him. She unzipped her uniform jacket and shed it, dropping it on the back of his favorite chair as she headed toward the kitchen. With one ear cocked toward the bedrooms, he padded barefoot after her. He should have gotten cold, standing there shirtless in the door while winter air swirled in, which also should have taken care of his obvious reaction to her. But no.

He started the coffeemaker and clicked on the baby monitor perched on the kitchen counter. Listening to liquid drip into the stainless-steel carafe, Deke faced Quin and leaned back against the counter, legs crossed at the ankles. He absentmindedly scratched his chest. Quin's sharp intake of breath reminded him that he had company. And that he was standing here mostly naked.

What would it take to get her mostly naked? *No, scratch that.* He wanted her completely naked. Or at least out of that dang bulletproof vest she wore. Yes, she needed the armor for her job, but he really wanted to see the woman beneath the uniform. Neither of them spoke until the coffeemaker signaled that caffeine was now available in hot liquid form. He poured two mugs and slid one across the island to his guest before he rummaged in the fridge for the vanilla creamer she liked. He'd bought a big bottle just for her.

After several deep gulps, Deke figured he was coherent enough to carry on a normal conversation—something more refined than "Happy hump day. Me man. You woman. Get in my bed. Now."

"So what brings you out here so early?"

Quin stared pointedly at the neon diner clock on the wall above his fridge. "Late night?"

Deke liked a snarky woman as much as the next guy, but this morning, it flat out irritated him. "As a matter of fact, yeah. The baby was sick. She didn't get down until almost five." He made a production of looking at the watch on his wrist. "I've had all of three and a half hours sleep."

Did she look contrite there for a whole second? If Deke had any sense at all—and according to his mother, that was a debatable question—he'd do everything possible to get this annoying, if sexy, woman out of his life and get on with things. He'd considered doing so, but something always distracted him. Noelle cried. His phone rang. Food needed to be cooked, dishes washed, naps. Besides, he was curious. About Quin. About…them.

"Sick?" Her voice sounded accusatory.

"According to Jolie, it was a touch of colic and something all babies get on occasion. Her solution was to bundle up Noelle, put her in the car seat and drive around until she fell asleep. I don't even want to talk about how many miles I put on my truck between one and five."

"You drove her around in your truck? In the middle of the night?"

Deke yawned and scratched his chest again while taking another swig of coffee. "Yeah, those are the same questions I asked Jolie. Since she is both a nurse *and* a mother, I figured she was the expert."

Quin's gaze was glued to his hand. He scratched again and then rubbed down his stomach. She looked a little glassy-eyed now. He'd considered stepping into the laundry room to grab a T-shirt, but given Quin's reaction to him being shirtless, he was now considering tugging his sleep pants just a little bit lower.

"Like what you see, Trooper Kincaid?" The words were out of his mouth before he thought about them, and maybe the lazy drawl in his voice was a bit of overkill, but Quin's reaction was immediate and sharp.

"You need to put on clothes, Mr. Tate."

And she needed to take some off. Color was surging into her cheeks, and he just couldn't resist poking at her. "My house, my rules."

She sputtered, her mouth opening and closing several times before she managed to speak. "That's it. We're done. There is no way this child should—"

Noelle's coughing and crying came through the monitor loud and clear. He automatically headed toward her room. Quin didn't follow him, but her voice did.

"Perhaps you aren't cut out to be the caretaker of

an infant, Mr. Tate. Why don't you give up this farce and just let me put her into foster care?"

And there she went again. Yeah, this time he would call Chance. Maybe.

Quin didn't feel like traipsing down the hall after Deke, who was ignoring her. She could hear the baby crying through the monitor. Moments later, the microphone picked up Deke's soothing voice.

"Shh, baby girl. S'okay now. I'm here. No need for tears. Are you hungry? Bet you need a fresh diappy, too. Let me check."

Quin heard the rustle of material and then a disgusted "whew-eee," followed by a low chuckle that did all sorts of things to her insides. That was so not fair. The man was changing a dirty diaper and she was plotting ways to get him to kiss her again.

"You are a sweet little stinky-butt, baby girl. Let's get you all clean now before we have to go see that mean ol' state trooper."

Was it her imagination or did Deke's voice get louder when he said that last part? Jerk. He probably knew she was listening to every word. She took back everything she'd just been thinking. She would sit here, finish her coffee, check the baby and skedaddle. She'd had quite enough of the egotistical man, standing around all seductive in those flannel pants showing off his tight abs and scratching through the just-enough-to-be-interesting thatch of dark hair on his chest, making her want to run her fingers through it. Nope. She. Was. Done.

Then he walked in with a dopey grin on his face

as he looked at the baby cradled in his arms. Men shouldn't get that look on their faces when dealing with small, squirmy humans. Heck, as far as she was concerned, *women* shouldn't go all googly-eyed, but they did. Deke ignored Quin as he settled the baby into a carrier on the counter. Noelle cooed at him as he prepped her bottle and clapped her hands when he took her out of the contraption and settled into his favorite chair in the great room.

Swiveling on her stool, Quin watched him. She had to admit the guy truly was competent. He changed diapers. He made bottles. Judging by the basket of neatly folded clothes in the laundry room behind the kitchen, he knew how to run a washer and dryer.

"Ha. He'll make some woman a great wife one of these days," she muttered. Not that she cared. She wasn't in the market for a wife. Or a husband. And especially not a boyfriend. Her biological clock could just keep tick-tick-ticking along. Home and hearth weren't high on her priority list. But… She glanced around.

Every time she came out here, she got the same feeling. This wasn't just another house to Deke. This was his home. He had a residence in Nashville—she'd checked, but this log cabin was home. She caught the chuckle bubbling up before it escaped. Calling this house a log *cabin* was like calling the Barron Hotel a motel. Even so, the place felt…lived in. Comfortable. A place where you could take your shoes off, plop your feet on the coffee table and watch TV.

She looked into the living area at the soaring ceilings, the huge windows that opened to breathtaking vistas, the massive native stone fireplace flanked by bookcases filled with books. Curious, she slipped off the stool and tiptoed over to check some of the titles. There seemed to be no rhyme or reason to his "filing" system, or the types of books on the shelves. She took down a biography of Harry Truman. It was obvious from the wear and tear on the pages that the book had been read. She reshelved it, checked the Harry Potter book next to the biography. It, too, looked well-read and disheveled. Like its owner.

Quin did not want to like Deacon. She didn't want this case to get personal in any way, shape or form. But it had, despite her best efforts. There was just something about the guy that sucked people in. Whether it was his good-ol'-boy demeanor, those amazing blue eyes or his handsome face. Not to mention that honed body... She jerked her thoughts back to business. Treading dangerous ground, she reminded herself.

"You're thinking awfully hard over there." The whiskey-rough sound of his voice startled Quin out of her ruminations. Was there anything *not* sexy about the man?

"Actually, I wasn't thinking anything except I've made my duty call and I should get on with my day."

"Suit yourself. I *was* going to offer breakfast..." Was he wheedling?

"Sorry. Already ate." Quin settled her belt and strode toward the chair. Where Deke was sitting. Leaning against her coat. "I'll just grab my coat." She indicated it with a tilt of her head.

"Ah. Sorry." Deke leaned forward but only far

enough that she could grab the collar and tug. He was such a jerk.

Yes. A jerk. Not a nice man. Not an aw-shucks country boy with blue eyes and a dimple. She needed to remember that if she was to get through this whole situation with her sanity intact. "Sorry I woke you. I'll try to schedule my visits a little later in the day, seeing as you aren't a morning person." Quin headed for the door. "I'll let myself out."

"Y'all come back now, hear?"

Was he mocking her? While she normally had a good ear for sarcasm, Quin couldn't tell. Yes, his drawl sometimes became more pronounced, but he did that to flirt, or win over an unsuspecting adversary. She was onto that particular shtick.

Don't look back. Don't look back. She couldn't help herself. She looked back. Deke had the baby up on his shoulder, patting her back. That so was not an image she wanted in her head on the drive back to Oklahoma City. Then the insufferable man looked up at her and winked.

The door slammed behind Quin and if the noise hadn't startled Noelle so that she cried and spit up some formula, Deke would have been totally satisfied by their interplay. She wanted him. And it irritated the snot out of her. Yup. She would share his bed before it was all said and done.

He pushed out of the chair and headed to the bathroom. Noelle needed a bath. He needed a shower. And then he had some work to do around the ranch. He had a crazy dream about Noelle, about teaching her to ride a horse. To play the guitar. She wasn't his. But she could be. Even if the paternity test turned out negative, adoption was an option.

What the hell was he thinking? He stared down at the baby splashing in the plastic tub secured to the broad granite slab covering the bathroom's vanity. Single parenting was hard—as he'd discovered while looking after her for almost a month. Still, Noelle owned a huge chunk of his heart. While easier, life without her would be so much lonelier, and he wondered if he truly wanted to go back to his life as it was before.

Noelle cooed at him and dang if she wasn't batting her eyelashes. She was a born flirt. The blue of her eyes was almost the same shade as Quin's. And though her fuzzy cap of hair was a pale gold, it might turn to a richer blond like the woman who'd just marched out of his house.

Wouldn't that be something.

Twelve

December was half over and Quin was so tired of making this drive. Coming out here to the ranch just added one more frustration to her day. She'd spent the morning peering over the shoulder of an Oklahoma State Bureau of Investigation agent and getting nothing but attitude for it. No one had been able to locate a birth certificate or any record of baby Noelle's birth. Without that, they had very little to go on in order to identify her mother.

The Chickasaw Tribal Police had assisted in getting security-cam footage of the parking lot. It pictured a young woman creeping up to the bus and depositing the basket, but her face was obscured. Quin had watched the footage over and over, noting the almost perfect timing between the mother leaving her baby and the appearance of the bus driver. Little more than a minute separated the two events.

She had lots of theories about the situation. Had the bus driver been in on it from the beginning? Who else would know the timing so precisely? Quin made a note to interview the man again. Then she wondered if the mother had been nearby, hiding and watching to make sure the baby was found quickly. If so, that indicated a level of caring. If not, then Quin would recommend termination of parental rights in absentia, clearing the way for the baby to go into foster care with a chance at adoption. She wasn't into kids but Noelle was a cute one. Some family would snap the baby up in a heartbeat.

Quin was honest enough to hope for as little time in foster care as possible. The vast majority of foster parents were wonderful, loving people doing their best for the kids shuttled through the system. Her own experiences weren't the norm.

All this was well and good, but living with a single superstar was not in the best interests of a little girl, no matter how rich the guy was, or how much power his family wielded. The whole situation still irritated her. She hated people who gamed the system, and from her observations, the Tates, with the assistance of the powerful Barrons, were masters at it. She'd bet dollars to doughnuts that they could have fast-tracked the DNA test but every time she asked for the results, Chance Barron, as Deacon's attorney, stonewalled.

The media had caught wind of the story and there was speculation. She'd fielded a few calls, answering questions with the ubiquitous "No comment." She had to assume that Deacon's "people" were doing the same.

To distract herself, she pulled through the drive-through of a fast-food restaurant and ordered lunch on the run: cheeseburger, salty fries and a big soft drink, plus a coffee for later. After receiving her order, she found a parking space at the edge of the lot, pulled in and scarfed down her food.

Sitting at a stoplight a short time later, Quin drummed her fingers on the steering wheel. She couldn't stall any longer—time to make the drive to the land of sexy singers. She shook her head and pressed the accelerator as the light changed to green. Deacon Tate was not sexy. Not to her. And that kiss they'd exchanged had meant nothing at all. Nada. She was a professional. And he was a pain in her…profession.

With Noelle down for her afternoon nap, Deke grabbed a fast shower, then got another cup of coffee and settled in his office to catch up on some work. Trying to schedule studio time around the tour had been a hassle. And now, with Noelle in his life, the thought of flying to Nashville didn't sit well. Maybe he'd invite the band to come back early. The guys could lay down some tracks in his home studio before their gig on New Year's Eve.

He sent out emails, along with pictures he'd snapped of Noelle. The munchkin was far too cute and she had him totally wrapped around her tiny fingers. Deke was man enough to admit that fact to himself and his family. He glanced at the calendar. Was it possible a month had passed since she'd come into his life? Was it possible to love a child who probably wasn't his as much as he'd come to love this one?

His phone dinged with an incoming text. Deke opened it and stared. He didn't want to fumble with letters on a screen. He wanted to hear his cousin's voice, needed the immediacy of a direct answer. He scrolled through his contacts, almost smiling when the first name on his VIP list was Chance Barron. What did it say about him that he called the cousin who was his attorney far more often than Chase, the cousin who ran Barron Entertainment and was technically his boss? When Chase had opened Bent Star Records, Deke was first in line to sign with the label.

His coffee cup was empty so he headed to the kitchen for a refill, hitting the call button on his cell as he walked. Chance picked up on the second ring and Deke put him on the speaker so he could pour his coffee.

"You answered quick. Are you in the middle of something?"

"No. In fact, you caught me between stuff, so excellent timing."

"Is it really done?" Deke asked bluntly. He'd been as nervous as a pimply-faced boy meeting his prom date's father waiting on Chance to work his legal magic.

"Yeah, cuz. It's done. You're officially good to keep her until after the New Year."

For the first time in several weeks, the pressure in Deke's chest eased and he inhaled deeply. "Thanks,

Chance." A brisk knock sounded on the door. Expecting his ranch foreman, Deke called, "It's open."

After a pause, Chance said, "Not a problem, Deke. You do know, though, that you can't keep her forever, right?"

Deke heard the other man blow out a breath. "You got the results back."

A long moment of silence had Deke fisting his hands before his cousin spoke. "Yeah. She's not yours. The test was conclusive."

A block of ice settled in his chest, but he breathed through it, the cold dissipated by a flash of fierce love for the little girl. He didn't want to give her up. "You're wrong, Chance. She *is* mine. If not by blood, then by heart. You need to figure out a way I can adopt her, so—"

"You can't do that!" The indignant voice cut him off midsentence, and Deke pivoted. Quin stood just inside the door all but vibrating with outrage.

With far more calmness than he felt, he said, "Do what you have to, Chance. I need to take care of something here."

"Yeah, I heard. Good luck with that, bud."

"What game are you playing, Mr. Tate?"

Mr. Tate? So she was back to using formality to keep him at arm's length. "Listen, Quin—"

"No. I'm through listening. I have no clue what sort of crazy publicity stunt you're staging but it's done. Your attorney just told you you're not the father. I'm taking the baby into custody and transferring her to

DHS for placement in foster care. *Real* foster care, with foster parents who have been licensed."

"The hell you are." Deke exhaled. Reached deep to find the calm he needed to deal with this maddening cop. It would really help if he wasn't so damn attracted to her.

She edged around him, and he saw the calculation in her eyes. She was trying to maneuver past him to get down the hallway to Noelle's room. That wasn't going to happen.

"Results of the paternity test don't matter at the moment, Quin. Custody papers have been signed by a judge and filed. I'm Noelle's temporary guardian until a formal hearing can be held in January."

"You aren't fit to take care of a baby."

He arched one brow and all but dared her to follow up on that allegation. When she didn't, he waited some more. One thing he'd learned while dealing with her— Quin Kincaid was long on righteous indignation but very short on patience. He planned to use that to his advantage. Until Noelle wailed.

Deacon was down the hallway leading to the bedrooms before Quin could do much more than take a step. As she arrived in the nursery, he already had the baby in his arms and was jostling her gently. He was not-so-subtly checking for a dirty diaper and then he had the little girl on the top of the dresser-cum-changing table.

Quin didn't know how to react to this...domesticity. Deacon Tate was a superstar. He had *people*, as in "I'll have my people call your people," but none of those people were here in this designer log house that felt homey and warm. And since none of them was there, he was the one changing the baby's diaper. And not for the first time. What guy did that? Plus, he constantly proved her wrong about his caretaking capabilities.

But why? What was in this deal for him? He wasn't necessarily a Nashville bad boy. Something of a flirt, with a different girl at every event, but not...*bad*. As far as her investigation revealed, there'd been no scandal associated with him. He didn't need to rehabilitate his image with an act of kindness like this. On paper, Deacon appeared to be a genuinely nice guy who did good things for people, even if he was a serial dater.

But Quin was a cynic, due to her own childhood in and out of the system. She'd been used as a pawn by a rich family and knew from first-hand experience. No one was this altruistic—not without a big payoff. There had to be some sort of perk for a star to take on an abandoned baby that wasn't his. Her head hurt from unraveling his motivation. All the possible reasons were more tangled up than a plate of angel-hair pasta.

And what was the deal with wanting to adopt Noelle? Yeah, since the kid wasn't his, was this just a big ruse to gain points with his adoring public? It wouldn't be the first time a big star adopted a kid and it got splashed all over the news.

She glanced up to discover Deacon standing in front of her. A moment later, he handed off the baby, whom she grabbed by sheer reflex.

"Hey!" she called after his retreating back.

"She's hungry. I'm going to fix her bottle." He paused and glanced over his shoulder at Quin. "Unless you want to fix the bottle?"

"No, that's okay. I'll—"

He walked away, effectively cutting off her protest.

As Quin followed him into the spacious kitchen, baby Noelle cooed and her tiny fingers tangled in Quin's ponytail. She smiled, despite herself, and jostled the kid the way she'd seen Deacon do. Settling one hip on the wrought-iron bar stool by the kitchen island, she watched the far-too-sexy man bustle about. He spooned formula into the bottle, added water, put on the lid and shook, whistling the whole time. It was a catchy tune, and Quin tried to place the song.

"You wanna feed her?"

She gulped and shook her head, resisting the urge to back away. "No. Sorry. Not the maternal type." She wasn't, but she wasn't petrified of holding the baby. When had that happened? When had she grown comfortable in this house with these two?

Deacon smiled. And darn if that smile shouldn't have been outlawed. Women around the world would do anything to be on the receiving end of that smile and here she was, sitting in the man's house, two feet away, trying hard to resist him.

"I'm not so sure about that, darlin'," he drawled. The light in his blue eyes was soft, like the sun kissing the sky a moment after dawn.

Nope. She wasn't falling for this. For him. Not at all. She was a cop. That was all she wanted to be. She didn't have room for superstar boyfriends and cute babies and Parade of Homes houses. And hadn't she just been upset with him? What was up with her seesawing emotions? Bad news all around.

"Quincy?" He whispered her name across her cheek in a warm breath. When she focused her eyes, he was close—too close. If-she-puckered-her-lips-they'd-be-kissing close.

"Yeah?" Oh, good grief. Was that her sounding all breathy and—and…girly?

"The baby's hungry, darlin'."

"Oh." She blinked several times before she leaned back and surrendered Noelle to Deacon.

He had a dish towel slung over his shoulder and his muscular biceps barely flexed as he settled Noelle in the cradle of one arm. Was it possible for the man's eyes to go even softer? The look on his face was… serene.

While she was contemplating his expression, he caught her off guard, and swooped in to kiss her. With a swirl of tongue between her lips. Sweet, gentle, but still hungry. She leaned away, mindful that he was holding the baby, not sure if she was upset or glad he'd kissed her. "Why did you do that?"

He grinned, totally unapologetic. "Because I needed to taste you again." He walked away and settled into his favorite chair, adjusted the baby and plopped the nipple of the bottle in her mouth. Noelle sucked noisily.

Argh. Quin wanted to wipe her mouth. Or rinse it with mouthwash to get rid of his taste. She leaned over, trying to listen surreptitiously. Was Deacon crooning to the baby? He was! He was singing to her. Quin couldn't help herself. She slid off the stool and crept closer to hear his voice.

"Rainbows and ponies, sweet baby mine. Ribbons and lace, to make you look fine. He'll dry your tears, kiss away your fears. He'll sing you lullabies. You are his sweetheart, his precious child. Sweet as can be, baby of mine. Daddy will love you to the end of time."

Daddy. What had Deacon told his cousin? *If not by blood, then by heart.* Quin couldn't help but feel a little jealous. He'd bonded with the baby. Quin had to admit that it would be tough to remove Noelle from Deacon's care.

Despite her reaction when she overheard the conversation with Chance Barron, something sweet settled inside her as she continued to watch man and baby. When the bottle was empty, Deacon shifted Noelle to his shoulder to rub and pat her back until the baby emitted a sleepy burp. What was the male equivalent of the Madonna and child? Because what Quin saw sitting in that chair on a frigid December day was every bit as powerful.

What was wrong with her? She couldn't have feelings for this man. She wasn't maternal so why should this image move her to sniffles and make her feel like someone had just punched her in the chest? She was a state trooper. Deacon and the baby were part of her investigation. That was all. They shouldn't be more. They *couldn't* be. And she'd make sure they wouldn't affect her. Oh, yeah. She'd get right on that.

Just as soon as she got her heart back under control.

Thirteen

Quin needed a vacation. Desperately. She was scheduled to leave in one day. The last thing she needed was to see Deacon. She went brain dead anytime he looked at her with those sleepy, sexy eyes of his. Or if his lips quirked up in that teasing smile. Or his mouth took hers like he was starving for the taste of her. No. She had to start thinking with her brain instead of her libido.

She was annoyed. At him. At his whole family. She needed to hang on to that feeling to do what she had to do.

Because there had been a break in the case.

Bridger Tate and Cash Barron had located Amanda Brooks, Noelle's mother. A caseworker from CPS and Quin were both there when the men questioned the girl. And she was *just* a girl—barely eighteen, the baby's father long gone. She'd made noises at first about Deacon being the father but Bridger shut that down when he asked about a birthmark. Amanda went into great detail describing it. Only problem? Deke didn't have one. Then Cash mentioned the DNA evidence—or lack thereof.

The teen had burst into tears and confessed she just wanted Noelle to have a wonderful life. Deacon was her favorite singer. The note and leaving Noelle at the bus had been a desperate, spur-of-the-moment action. CPS's unwritten mission was to keep families together. While a tour bus didn't strictly fit the guidelines of Oklahoma's Baby Safe Haven law where a parent could leave an infant in an approved facility like a fire station without legal repercussions, the teen's intention had been to keep her baby safe. No one was inclined to prosecute though the CPS worker wanted the baby in state foster care while Amanda took parenting classes.

Bridger and Cash weren't on board with that plan. Quin recalled the conversation she'd overheard between Deke and Chance about adoption. The teenager didn't stand a chance against the power and wealth wielded by Deacon and his extended family.

And that had seemed to be confirmed when Amanda called the CPS worker first thing that morning and said she was voluntarily giving up her parental rights so Deacon could adopt Noelle. Quin had seen the writing on the wall as soon as the social worker called. Private adoption or not, Deacon shouldn't just get his way, and Quin was glad the state was stepping in. CPS was requesting an emergency hearing to terminate Deacon's temporary custody. Though Quin had seen how much he cared for Noelle, when people threw their money and influence around like that, it just plain ticked her off.

Today would be the last time she had to lay eyes on the irritating man. She had plane tickets. She had hotel reservations. And she was leaving tomorrow morning no matter what. Five-star resort. Sexy ski…what did one call the guys who hung out on the slopes? They definitely weren't ski *bunnies*, and ski bums seemed as derogatory as bunnies. Ah, well. She didn't care. In just over twenty-four hours, she would be ensconced in front of that roaring fire, aperitif in hand, admiring the beautiful people.

Speaking of beautiful people, she segued back into cursing Deacon under her breath. She did not want to see him. Or give him the chance to kiss her again. She *didn't*, despite what her libido whispered in her ear. That was why she'd tried to call. She'd made arrangements for someone else to do the welfare checks until Noelle was removed from Deacon's custody, and wanted to tell him to expect the CPS caseworker. She'd left messages to call her when he didn't answer the landline or his cell. Then she'd gotten worried. What if he'd gotten word of what was coming? Had he packed up the baby and run?

That was stupid. Just like her nagging worry that something had happened to him. That he'd slipped and fallen in the shower and was bleeding to death. Or was unconscious and drowning. All of which was totally ridiculous and she knew it. If she'd thought about the situation with any clarity, she would have just called his cousin-slash-attorney. She could still do that. Except...

Okay, so she might have a soft spot for the kid. And Deacon, idiot that Quin was. Tomorrow, she'd be on a plane and wouldn't return to duty for seventeen days. By then, she would have gotten Deke out of her system, and the whole baby thing would be in the hands of CPS and the lawyers. By the time she was back in Oklahoma, Deke would have found some other woman to torment. And kiss. Awesome. Just as long as it wasn't her. Because kissing him was just...

The back wheels on her cruiser squiggled as she pressed the brake pedal while approaching a stop sign. She'd been driving through a light fall of sleet and now hard little balls of sneet—a combination of snow and sleet—were bouncing against her windshield. Great. The polar express wasn't supposed to arrive in full force until *after* her flight left in the morning.

Seeing there was no traffic in either direction, Quin squirted through the intersection without coming to a full stop on the black ice in her lane. Why take a chance? She had better places to be and far better things to do. Luckily, half a mile farther on, she lost the asphalt pavement and hit gravel. For once, she didn't grouse about the state of the road. Gravel gave her better traction in the frozen precipitation.

As she turned onto the long, winding lane leading up to Deacon's house, she had a white-knuckled grip on the steering wheel. The windshield wipers were working overtime to clear the thick, fluffy flakes now falling. Great. Just...great. She would have her conversation with Deacon, check on the baby and get her tail home. She might even call the airlines to see if she could grab a flight out today. Just in case.

The snow drifting from the leaden skies was sticking to the ground and the temperature was dropping. Quin shivered despite her bulletproof vest and quilted nylon duty jacket. She parked near the front door and bolted onto the porch before adjusting her duty belt lower on her hips.

"Don't go in. Tell him he needs to answer his freaking phone. Make sure he and the baby are okay. Leave. Easy peasy."

Quin glanced over her shoulder. The snow was coming down heavier and the wind picked up. She knocked. And waited. She pounded. And waited. She tried the door. Locked. She was shivering now and debating returning to her car to grab gloves and her knit cap. She banged on the window. Waited. She returned to the front door. Her fist connected with the wood, the door opened and she all but fell into the warmth of the house.

"Quin? What are you doing out here?" Deacon looked surprised to see her. The baby was curled against his right shoulder, peeking out shyly.

"I've been trying to contact you all morning. Don't you ever answer the phone?"

He looked a little sheepish. "Noelle and I were down in the barn getting the animals settled before the storm."

Okay, maybe, that was a good excuse but... "You didn't answer your cell, either."

"Ah..." He shrugged and turned on his very lethal

good-ol'-boy smile, complete with dimple. "Left it up here at the house—"

"Yeah, yeah, whatever," she interrupted. "You should call Chance."

"Chance my attorney or Chance my cousin?"

"Aren't they one and the same?"

"Yes…and no." He chuckled. "If I'm in trouble, he's my attorney. If everything is copacetic, he's my cousin."

"You people think you have it all figured out, don't you?" Quin was frozen to the bone, frustrated and angry—as much with herself as with Deacon. "Your inability to remember to stick your phone in your pocket necessitated me driving out here. In a storm. To make sure you weren't dead or something." Why had she added that last bit? This was why she should have turned around and left as soon as she saw that he and the baby were fine.

Deacon looked her over and tilted his head toward the massive stone fireplace, where a fire was burning cheerily. "Go sit on the hearth and get warm. I'll put Noelle in her crib and get you some coffee. Then you can tell me why you were worried about us."

Quin opened her mouth to argue but he was already halfway to the kitchen. She was still shivering so she moved closer to the fire. A few minutes wouldn't hurt, right?

Deacon returned carrying a large, steaming mug. She accepted it and took an experimental taste. Just the right temperature, just sweet enough with a hint of vanilla cream. How did the guy remember that?

The heat radiating from the fireplace felt good on her back as she swallowed several long sips. She found herself oddly relaxed. The place smelled of cinnamon and pine, though there was no sign of a Christmas tree or other holiday accoutrements.

Quin was falling under his spell again. She had to stop this. "Christmas is less than a week away. Not doing the decorating thing?" She sounded snippy. That was good. No sexy, kissy thoughts about this man. Staying irritated. That was the key.

"Decorating?"

"Never mind. The sooner this is done, the sooner I can get back to regular duty. This is my last day before vacation."

"Big plans?"

"Yes. I'm flying to Aspen for a ski vacation."

"With your boyfriend?"

"I don't have one. Not that it's any of your business." The man had kissed her and he was just now getting around to asking if she was attached?

"So…you're spending Christmas in a hotel?"

"Again, not your business."

"Fine. Sorry for being curious. Have fun, but I think you'll be surprised how lonely it can be."

"Lonely? The resort is booked full. Hard to be lonely with a lot of people around."

"*Hmmm.* Of course. All those families and couples. Fun times."

"You don't have a clue. Maybe I booked a singles package," she snapped.

He nodded sagely and made that *hmmm* sound in his throat again.

"Look, I'm not here to discuss my private life."

Deacon raised his arms in symbolic surrender. "Sorry. I thought we were friends."

"We can't be friends. This is my job."

"Are you always so blunt?"

"I'm a cop. It's part of the job description."

"Good to know."

"You still didn't answer my question about Christmas." And she was prolonging this conversation why? Because she couldn't help the insane curiosity teasing her brain.

"I'll do a tree but we always gather at Mom's. The whole clan. Big ranch breakfast then stockings and presents. We eat a massive turkey dinner with all the trimmings, and promptly fall into food comas." He sipped his coffee, one hip leaning against the back of the huge leather chair. "I'm not always home, though. In the early years, we were usually on the road. I've spent more than a few Christmases in a hotel room. Trust me, being home is way better."

"Easy for you to say," she muttered. Her parents and their on-again-off-again marriage were a hot mess. Holidays spent with her four brothers in and out of the foster-care system didn't engender fond memories. Even now, as adults, they weren't very close. And just that quickly, her temper was back.

Quin needed to wrap this up and hit the road before she said or did something totally inappropriate. Like kiss that smug smile off Deacon's face. Wait. No. She had no desire to get that close to him, with his shaggy hair hanging in his eyes just begging her fingers to brush it away, and those lips curling on one side, teasing her. She shook her head and defaulted to gulping down the rest of her coffee. She'd been there, done that, and wasn't about to do it again.

Because if she surrendered to the need building in her, she wouldn't leave. And even worse, she'd forget that this man was someone she didn't like.

Her phone pinged with a text, saving her from falling further down that rabbit hole. Quin retrieved it from her coat pocket and read the message. The pickup order had been delayed until after Christmas.

"You must be charmed," she said, reading him the text. So what if her sarcasm came out to play. The stars always aligned for people like Deacon, and if she had his luck, she'd go to Thunder River Casino and make a fortune. She headed toward the kitchen to deposit her mug. Time to hit the road.

"It's really coming down out there. Why don't you stay until there's a break in the weather? I was just about to make breakfast. Stay. Eat with me."

He'd walked up behind her, catching her unaware. Which freaked her out a little. She was very proud of her situational awareness, and the fact that he could sneak up on her was unsettling. She glanced out the huge window over the sink and blanched. The ground—what she could see of it through the snow now blowing horizontally—was covered in white swirls.

"I can't. I have to get back to Oklahoma City."

Deacon crowded her up against the counter. Why

did he have to smell so good? Like almond, sage and lemon. The mug clattered in the huge farmhouse sink behind her, and her phone landed on the granite counter.

"I'm a really good cook." He seduced her with the dimple again. "Mom made sure all us boys could look after ourselves."

Quin snorted in disbelief. "Yeah, right."

"I even know how to sew. Do laundry. Pick up after myself. Put the toilet seat down." He winked and her insides melted. He was a rich jerk but a charming one. Still, she had plans, and her duty to do. Standing here wondering if he would try to kiss her again was not on her agenda.

"Good for you. I've made sure you and the baby were breathing. I need to hit the road." Squaring her shoulders, she announced, "The CPS caseworker will do welfare checks from here on out." She ducked past him and hustled toward the door. Deacon still managed to beat her and open it for her, ever the gentleman. He gave her a piercing look but said nothing about her announcement.

A blast of frigid wind lashed her face, and she hesitated. Snow had built up on her windshield and she'd have to brush it away before driving. Squaring her shoulders, she dove into the teeth of the storm.

"Get in the car and get it started," Deacon yelled above the howling wind. "Get warm. I'll get the windows."

She was already shivering so didn't pause to argue. He donned a heavy sheepskin jacket and was pulling on gloves. The cruiser started—thankfully. As soon as the temperature gauge climbed above C, she hit the heater and defroster full-blast.

Deacon didn't just clear her windshield, he knocked the snow off all the windows and stomped down the snow in front of her tires. Then he stood back and saluted. She rolled her eyes but gave him a wave as she put the car in gear and slowly pulled out.

Once she turned onto the section line road, she was fighting snowdrifts. The road ran directly east and west while the wind came from due north. The windshield wipers barely kept up and she caught herself hunching over the steering wheel to peer through the windshield.

Quin wasn't sure when she realized there were ruts in the road. They were too wide for her cruiser but she could put one set of wheels into the tire track and follow it. She concentrated on staying in the rut.

Something dark and huge loomed up in front her. Out of reflex, Quin hit the brakes and jerked the wheel to the left. Her actions sent the car into a dizzying spin. She fought the centrifugal gravity created by the out-of-control vehicle. The car came to an abrupt stop. She slammed her head against the window and tried to breathe around the air bag as the car engine sputtered and died.

The bag eventually deflated and Quin took stock of her situation. She could sum it up in one word: bad. She reached for the radio and got nothing but static. Same with the MDT, the mobile data terminal. Her phone was in her pocket. No worries. She'd call Dispatch and they could send a wrecker for her. Except her phone wasn't *in* her coat pocket. Or any of her pockets. She unhooked the shoulder harness and banged her shoulder on the driver's-side door. That's when she realized the car was tilted at a crazy angle.

Running her hand over the floor, she couldn't locate her phone. Then she remembered. She'd set it down on the kitchen counter at Deke's. And in her fit of self-preservation, she'd walked off without it. She was stuck in the middle of nowhere in the blizzard of the century with no way to call for help.

Quin breathed through her initial panic. Her head was pounding but she was a trained professional. She'd been following tracks made by a tractor or road grader or something. They'd come back. Find her. If her car wasn't buried in a snowdrift by then. How far had she driven? A mile? Two? She'd been driving slowly so she couldn't be too far from Deke's. She'd just have to walk back to his house. The idea grated on her but she had little choice. She had gloves. A warm hat. She was tough. She could do this.

Squirming so she could reach around the MDT mounted between the seats, she snagged the passenger door handle and shoved. Nothing happened. Moving into a better position, she pushed again, using both hands. Still nothing.

After ten minutes, Quin considered using her pocketknife to hack away the air bag so she could wrap up in it. She could see her breath and her fingers were going numb.

"Quin!"

Was someone shouting?

"Quin! Are you in there?" Someone pounded on the passenger door. No, not just someone—Deke.

"Deke! I'm here. I'm here!"

Metal groaned and then the door opened a crack.

"Thank God. Hang on, darlin'. I'll have you out in a flash."

He had something in his hands, like a long crowbar, and he forced the passenger door to open wider. He leaned in and offered her his gloved hands.

"Grab hold, Quin. I'll pull you out."

A small, feminist part of her rebelled, but her teeth were chattering too hard to speak. She grabbed his hands. He lifted her like she weighed nothing. Then she was in his arms and he was carrying her to a beast of a four-wheel-drive pickup. Depositing her in the passenger seat, he slammed the door shut and hustled around to climb in the driver's side.

"Wh-wh-what are y-you d-doing here?"

"Rescuing you, obviously."

Damn his dimple, but he was bundling her into a blanket and the heater was blowing.

"You forgot your phone. Soon as I realized it, I grabbed up Noelle and headed out. I figured to catch up to you before you hit the highway. Appears I did."

"You dragged the baby out in this? What if you wrecked? That's just plain stupid!"

He stared at Quin, dimple and eye twinkles gone. "I'm more prepared for this weather than you, *Trooper*."

She bristled at the emphasis on her title. She was prepared. Sort of. She had a kit in the trunk—which she couldn't reach after sliding off the road. In her defense, every meteorologist in the state had missed the sudden arrival and escalation in the power of the storm.

He continued, "For your information, she's in this flannel sack thing and wrapped in a Pendleton blanket with the heater running full-blast. Fast asleep, I might add. I also have extra blankets, water, food, a candle—you did know that a big candle will heat a cab this size, right? I wasn't about to leave her at home alone. That's what stupid people do and I'm not stupid, despite what you continue to believe."

Okay, he had a point there. Leaving the baby alone would have been worse than dragging her outside and this huge truck seemed more than capable of tackling even the highest snowdrifts.

"Where would you be if I hadn't come along? It's not like this road is well-traveled in *good* weather. An Oklahoma blue norther with a side of blizzard? Most sane folks are snug at home riding out the storm. Which is where we're headed. Home."

Fourteen

The tracks his truck had made on the way to find Quin were quickly filling in as Deke drove back to the house. Turning around had been an exercise in caution and he'd almost given up, deciding it might be easier to just back up the mile they had to go. But he persevered. By the time they reached his place, Quin had stopped shivering, but she had a nasty knot on her head and he was worried.

He nosed the big vehicle in as close to the back door as he could. This area provided more shelter from the storm, as it was on the south side of the house. He squeezed Quin's arm to get her attention. She gazed at him, her eyes a little glassy. Not good. He'd have to check her for signs of concussion once they got inside.

"I'm going to take Noelle in, then I'll come back

to get you. I'll leave the truck running for the heat. Okay?"

Quin blinked several times as if trying to remember where she was. "Oh. Yeah. That makes sense. I'll just get out and come with you."

"No, darlin'. Just stay in the truck. The snow's deep even if we're out of the wind. If you slip or anything, I can't help you while I'm carrying the baby. Just sit tight. Okay?"

"Okay. Yes. That makes sense."

She was repeating herself and his worry ratcheted up a notch. He had another electronic key in the house in case Quin managed to lock the doors while he was moving Noelle inside. The baby yawned as he got her, still wrapped and strapped into the carrier, out of the car-seat base. He slammed the truck door and waded through the growing snowdrifts to the service door. He set the baby carrier down in the mudroom and trudged back to the truck. When he opened the passenger side door, Quin all but fell into his arms. He got her hitched up into a princess carry and bumped the door with his hip to close it.

He slipped and almost went down but found his balance before he dumped either of them in the snow. Inside the house, Deke set Quin on her feet, made sure she was steady and turned to click the remote start key fob to turn off the truck. He had to sweep out a small pile of snow to shut the door. With the door latched against the wind, Deacon stripped off his gloves and coat and hung them on the wall rack in the mudroom. Luckily, he'd already fed and watered the horses. They'd be able to weather the storm. Matt had rounded up the small herd of cattle and secured them in a secondary barn before holing up in his own house.

"C'mon, darlin'. Let's get you warm, 'kay? And I want to take a look at your head."

"My head?" Quin reached up with trembling fingers, but he snagged her hand before she touched the bump.

"Yeah, don't think you want to touch it, sweetheart. You've got a whale of a lump on your forehead. Do you remember what happened?"

She squinted her eyes as she thought. "Uh-huh. I was following a track. The snow was so thick I was watching the road right at the end of my hood. I looked up and there was something big blocking the way. I…" Color crept up her cheeks. "I made a rookie mistake. I hit the brakes and jerked the wheel."

"I didn't see anything in the road." He shook his head as she started to argue. "Hon, you were in the bar ditch for a while before I got there. Whatever that vehicle was, the driver probably never even knew you were behind him. C'mon. Get out of your coat. I'll take a look at your head."

An hour later, Quin was soaking in the whirlpool tub in the master bedroom, Noelle was in her automatic swing cooing happily and Deke had fielded phone calls from every female member of his extended family. Diapers. Check. Food and formula. Check. Backup generator. Check. Weather report: blizzard conditions, lots of snow. Check. Sexy woman naked in his tub. Double check. Eventually, she'd have to call her supervisor to explain the situation. She wasn't going anywhere until the storm blew itself out.

He made a fresh pot of coffee, then headed to his closet. Quin couldn't wear her uniform the whole time she was here. And as much as he'd appreciate the view of her in the robe hanging on the back of the bathroom door—a robe he'd never worn—Quin would need real clothes. He found a selection of sweats, tees and jeans that might fit and laid them out on the bed. The idea of Quin wearing his clothes was a real turn-on, not that he needed any encouragement in that department.

The bathroom door opened a crack, and Deke caught a glimpse of Quin's face. "Feeling warmer now?"

"Yes. Thanks."

"You found the robe on the door?"

"Yes."

"I laid out some clothes for you to try on. Weather guys say we're stuck for at least forty-eight hours. Considering where I live, it'll probably be longer before a plow can get through." He wasn't about to mention the bulldozer stored in his equipment barn.

"No. Just nooo." The bathroom door closed and a *thunk* followed.

Deke rushed to the door and tried the handle. It turned but wouldn't open. "Quin? Are you okay in there?"

"No. I'm supposed to get on a plane tomorrow. I have reservations. Colorado. Skiing. Luxury resort. Remember?"

Deke worked to keep the laughter out of his voice as he said, "Hon? There won't be any planes in or out of Will Rogers Airport and Colorado is getting hammered by this same weather system."

"Great. Just…great."

He thought it was. Quin under his roof for an indeterminate period of time? Check. A chance for her to get to know him? Check. A chance to get her into his bed? Double check.

Quin hid in the bathroom—and what a bathroom it was, with a huge whirlpool tub, a shower big enough for six and a heated floor. The fluffy robe hanging on the hook swamped her but it would do. After a few minutes of silence, she opened the door a crack and peeked out. Deke was nowhere to be seen and the bedroom door had been closed.

She was in the process of holding a pair of soft, faded jeans up to her waist when Deke tapped on the door. Quin clutched the robe closed and held her breath. The door didn't open as Deke's muffled voice filtered through the wood.

"Feel free to go through the dresser and my closet. Grab whatever you need."

"Thank you," she called back. She had one pair of panties and the sports bra she wore under her uniform. Unless the guy was a real pervert and he kept fan *souvenirs*, she doubted he'd have any lingerie stashed in his drawers. But if he was a boxer kind of guy, she could improvise. Because there was no way in the world she was going commando with Deacon around. He was lethal to the female libido. She wanted as many layers as she could pile on.

Not that she was afraid of him. Nope. Not at all. It was *her* reaction to the man that was terrifying. He made her stupid when his dimple appeared. And when he sang to the baby? She swore she could feel it in her womb and her biological clock jangled like an old-fashioned alarm clock.

Wearing a pair of his boxers—and she so wasn't going to think about the intimacy of that—Quin tried on the pair of jeans she was holding. They fit surprisingly well, if a little loose in the waist so that they rode lower on her hips than she was used to. She snagged a white T-shirt, shrugged into it and followed up with a baggy sweatshirt on top.

Armored in borrowed clothes, she ventured into the main part of the house. The baby was rocking in a swing contraption, eyes closed, one fist in her mouth. Deke had changed out of his wet jeans and now wore a dry pair slung low on his hips, topped by a T-shirt that molded to his chest and arms like a second skin. How was he not freezing?

Deke turned around, and a slow smile creased his cheeks. That was so not fair. Quin struggled to control her breathing and heart rate.

"I started some soup. Hope you like grilled cheese sandwiches."

Dark came early while they waited on the soup. The wind continued to howl and the snow drifted higher around the windows. This entire day had been a disaster. She stared out the window at the swirling snow. Deke appeared beside her.

"Want to decorate the tree after we eat?"

"Seriously?"

"Yeah. It's in the mudroom and I'd already dragged the decorations out of the attic. I haven't put up a tree in years but I really want one now." His dimple flashed at her as he smiled.

She hadn't put up a tree in her condo in…never. Decorating with Deacon sounded like fun. "Okay, sure."

The soup was hot, the grilled cheese gooey; the simple meal was oddly filling. She offered to do dishes while Deacon brought in the tree and got it set up.

He opened a box of ornaments and she admired the collection nestled on cotton batting. "Wow."

"Mom got these for me to celebrate my first concert tour. There's an ornament for each city we played."

Deke opened a plastic crate and found the tree lights. "Ah, good. Let's hope they work." He plugged them in and sure enough, the entire string lit up. She continued unpacking ornaments while he wound the lights through the branches of the Scotch pine.

When he stood back to admire his work, Quin couldn't help but tease him. "Don't you think there's a hole there on the left?"

He narrowed his gaze, studying the tree. "Where?"

Quin got up and pointed to a spot. "There." Then she moved the string up one branch. She backed away and nodded. "Perfect."

Deacon laughed and shook his finger. "I see what you did there."

As they decorated, Deke stopped to reminisce about some of the ornaments. Quin suspected each one had a story because they were all unique, but some seemed extra special to him. When the last one, a blown-glass New Orleans street car, was placed on the tree, Deacon reached for a small wooden box he'd set aside.

"Here," he said, handing it to her. Inside was another original—a hand-painted porcelain angel.

Quin was almost afraid to touch the delicate tree-topper. "She's lovely."

"I found her in a little shop in San Antonio."

She glanced up at the warmth in his voice. Quin made to hand it back but Deke shook his head. "Nope. The honor is yours. Up you go."

Before she knew what he had in mind, she was sitting on his shoulders, angel in her hand. She could just reach the very top of the tree to get the angel firmly clamped and braced. When Deke lowered her to the floor, his arm slipped around her shoulders as they gazed at the tree. She noticed that he'd arranged lights at the crown of the tree to highlight the angel.

"Beautiful."

"Yes, she is."

That was when Quin realized he was looking at her, and his expression sent shivers through her.

Day three of my captivity, Quin thought, the unspoken words sounding wry in her head. Despite the sexual tension that was so thick they could swim through it, she and Deke were getting along. She'd discovered he was funny, with a dry sense of humor. He was patient, as evidenced by the way he dealt with Noelle. And he was a talented musician. He'd serenaded her several times while she was curled up on the couch with a book. She couldn't remember the last time she'd read for pleasure.

The storm still showed no signs of losing its bluster. The electricity had flickered a time or two, but held steady. Deke assured her that the emergency generator would keep lights on and the fridge running if they lost power. At the moment, she was flipping through channels on the TV that dominated one wall of the great room. Deke was puttering around in the kitchen.

One of the daytime talk shows caught her attention when a picture of Deacon flashed on the screen and she paused to watch. What the five women were saying was just…drivel. And patently untrue.

She called to him. "You don't deserve this. To be paid back for your kindness with headlines and innuendos like these?" Quin glowered at the talking heads chatting on TV.

Deacon handed her a cup of hot chocolate with whipped cream and a chocolate-dipped pretzel for a stir stick. Dropping to the couch beside her, he tasted his coffee before answering. His voice held the shrug his shoulders hadn't made.

"It's how they make their living, Quin. I'm fair game." He looked mischievous and added, "Besides, they're staking out the Nashville condo because Bent Star leaked that I'd be spending the holidays there."

"Smart. But what they're saying still isn't fair."

Laughing, he said, "Neither is the fact I have to get out in the snow, trudge to the barn and feed the horses."

"Can't your foreman do that?"

Deke's brow furrowed and he looked genuinely puzzled. "Why would I make him get out in the cold to drive over here, and do something I can do quicker and easier? They're my horses. My responsibility."

Quin leaned back, studied him with her cop senses turned on. He truly didn't understand why she'd think he'd do anything else. This man had depths she was only beginning to fathom. That should scare her just a bit. Okay, a lot. She didn't want a relationship. Didn't want the complications or the investment—of time *or* emotion. And she certainly didn't want him to kiss her again. No way.

When Noelle fussed from where she lay in a portable playpen-and-crib contraption, Deacon was up and striding to her before Quin could even process there was a problem. She watched him pick up the infant and soothe her with the sweet lullaby he'd written just for the baby.

That darn biological clock kept right on ticking, sounding like the alarm clock the Peter Pan crocodile had swallowed. Tick. Tock.

After changing and resettling Noelle, Deke plopped back on the couch and realized Quin was still watching that dumb talk show.

Her head tilted as she focused on him. He resisted the urge to squirm under her scrutiny. Then she asked, "You really don't care?"

"What is it the kids say these days? Haters gonna hate?"

"Something like that."

"I'm in the public eye, Quin. There are always rumors and innuendos. This deal about the baby is just one more. I don't pay much attention. That's why record company PR people make the big bucks."

She laughed, and Deke wanted to hear her do that more often. The sound was bright and shiny, like the Christmas lights he'd strung on the tree. He'd enjoyed decorating the tree with Quin. With her and Noelle in the house, the place felt like Christmas, felt like a real home. Not wanting to fully acknowledge that, he tuned back into the conversation.

"So, you aren't a social-media addict like so many of the celebrities?"

It was his turn to laugh, though he exaggerated a grimace. "I'm told I have a Twitter account. But seriously? A hundred and forty characters? Does that include spaces and periods?"

"I guess this means I probably can't stalk you on Facebook, either."

"There's a fan page for the band, but no, I'm not on there." Deke scratched his head and pushed hair off his forehead. "I'm pretty much a country boy. I mean—" He swept a hand around the room. "Not exactly Beverly Hills standards."

"Oh, I don't know. Looks luxurious to me. And even though we're snowed in, the house still has electricity. Heat. And most important from a cabin-fever standpoint, cable TV. That makes you special."

Deke wanted to make Quin feel special, and he wanted to taste her again. He leaned forward and without thinking too deeply about his intentions, said, "I'm going to kiss you now."

"Are you asking or telling?"

"Yes."

Fifteen

Deke didn't need to hear Quin's sharp intake of breath to know her answer. Her hands were already reaching for him. He dipped his head, caught her bottom lip between his teeth and nipped. Then he kissed her slowly and gently, but very, very thoroughly. As long as the baby stayed asleep, he had all the time in the world to seduce this woman.

Her fingers clutched his shoulders as her body tensed, even though her lips softened against his. She was such a study of opposites and he couldn't wait to explore every last inch of her. He released her mouth, found the spot on her neck where her pulse beat rapidly. Deke wanted to strip her down, spread her and enjoy her in every way.

He didn't have to be told to go slow as he leashed his

own urgency. This was not the time. He'd take it slow and easy, like teasing a tune out of his guitar. That was the key. He would learn to play this woman.

She'd slept under his roof for two nights, though upstairs in the long-unused guest suite. They'd spent the days like an old married couple. They watched TV. Read. He played and sang to her and Noelle. Quin napped on the couch, her head resting on his thigh. He smiled against her skin. It had taken everything in him to not laugh out loud the first time she'd awakened in that position.

Deke returned to her mouth and kissed her deeply again, his tongue probing and tasting. She broke the kiss and leaned back. Her expression was serious as she studied him. Snagging one of her hands, he lifted it to his mouth, kissed each one of her fingers.

"If you could see yourself, Quin, with tousled hair and lips wet and swollen from my kiss."

That startled a laugh out of her. "Seriously? Where do you come up with this stuff?"

"Is it working?"

"No!" She was adamant but her eyes crinkled around suppressed laughter.

Winking, he pulled her close again and murmured against her lips, "I think it is."

She melted against him as he kissed her again. Emotions surged through him, feelings he wasn't sure he wanted to take out and examine very closely. The woman could get under his skin all too easily— already had, he realized. These last few days had shown him what he'd been missing. It was like life had just slapped him upside the head with a clue-by-four.

Deke didn't want to seduce Quin for the sake of having sex. Oh, no. It was far more complex than that. He wanted to make love to her. He eased her down on the couch, one hand teasing up the hem of the sweatshirt she wore. Calloused fingertips encountered smooth skin and he hardened. He wanted her naked and in his bed. Quin pressed her hands against his chest and pushed. He froze.

"What are we doing?" she whispered.

"If my mother had her way, I'd be a gentleman and say we were just making out. But I'm not a gentleman. I want you, Quin. I want you in my bed. I want to be *in* you."

She laid back against the cushions. "I have a duty—"

"Yes. To yourself. Do you want this to happen, Quin? If you say you don't, I'll get up and go take the next of many cold showers. I won't be happy. Damn, woman. Being cooped up in here with you has been torture." Deke sat up, knowing they needed to talk this through.

"When I first saw your car in that ditch? I couldn't breathe. I almost couldn't think. I was so damn scared that I'd find you really hurt." He swallowed hard. "Or worse. If you'd died… But you didn't. And I brought you home, darlin'. Not to my house, but home. Because that's what it feels like with you here."

She started to speak, but he silenced her with another quick, hard kiss. "Let me finish. Please."

He waited, holding his breath. Once he'd opened

the gate on his emotions, there was no way to stop
the stampede. Maybe he should have held back, taken
time to examine his feelings, but it was too late. Quin
nodded, looking uncertain, but he could deal with un-
certainty. Deke breathed, his lungs burning from the
infusion of oxygen.

"I know what you think of me—or what you used
to think. You've had a chance to get to know me. I've
been gettin' to know you since that night we met, stan-
din' in the cold in the parking lot at Thunder River. You
drive me crazy. So uptight. Proper. Even back then, I
wanted to take your hair down, see if it was as soft as
it looked. I wanted to tangle my fingers in it and kiss
you senseless. Damn, darlin', I think I've been hard for
you since I looked up and you announced, 'I'm Trooper
Kincaid. What's going on here?'"

Quin bit her lip to keep from smiling and he gave in
to the temptation to kiss her again. Her mouth opened
for his questing tongue. His hand cupped her cheek
and stayed after he broke the kiss.

"I've seen you every day since then. You've pissed
me off. You've driven me crazy with your scent and
your smile and being too cute even when you didn't
know you were being cute. You've made me laugh. And
you've made me want things only you can give me."

Deke shifted, grasped her and lifted her into his
lap. "Do you know how hard it's been for me to keep
my hands off you? The past two nights, I've climbed
the stairs and stood outside your door like a lovesick
hound. I listen to you breathe through the door and I

wonder if you're really sleepin' or if you're thinking about me, about us making love."

He paused and gazed into her eyes, didn't like what he saw there. "You're gonna run." She stiffened, pushed away, but he tightened his embrace. "Your feelings haven't changed? Tell me, Quin. Put me out of my misery. Is there any hope?"

A sob gathered in her chest, struggled to escape from her throat. If she let it, she'd never be able to stop the ones threatening to follow. She didn't want this tidal wave of emotion flooding her senses. *Home.* That word had arrowed into her heart. What did she know of healthy relationships? And how could this man, this superstar with all the talent and money and women in the world, want *her*? She was a cop, and far from beautiful. Nothing more. Nothing less.

His hands cupped her face, holding her so she had to look at him. Feeling the heat from his palms, the rough touch of his fingertips against her cheeks, she saw. This wasn't a game. This wasn't a seduction—well, okay, maybe it was, but he wanted *her*. Every instinct she'd had pointed to that conclusion. He wasn't lying. About any of this.

Could she let go? He definitely turned her on and from the first, her feelings had bounced around from frustration, anger, doubt, humor, lust—lots and lots of that—and plain old affection. She *liked* him. Too much. And she desired him.

Quin wanted to surrender to her feelings, wanted to give in to the demands of her own body. *Take me,* she silently begged. *Love me and don't ever let me go.* Because if they did this? If he ever let her go, she'd never recover.

As if he heard her silent pleas, he gathered her in his arms and stood. How strong was this guy? Her breath hitched and she pressed her lips to his throat. His arms tightened and his step quickened.

"In my bed, Quin. Okay?" he asked against her hair, raising goose bumps.

"Yes."

He settled them on the bed, both still clothed. She rested against a pile of pillows and in a crazy moment, given the circumstances, realized he'd made his bed that morning. She laughed, and loved the way his gaze softened as he watched her. Then he began to stroke her. His hands were gentle, at once teasing and soothing, as if he was seeking to both give and receive comfort.

"So beautiful, darlin'," he whispered over and over as his questing hands found her skin. A moment later, he whipped the sweatshirt over her head and she lay bare. She tensed until she saw his face. Heat surged in her blood and she flushed. He meant his words. She *was* beautiful in his eyes. She relaxed, ready to accept him.

His lips were firm when they found hers, after kissing their way along her shoulder, neck and cheek. He took the kiss deep, but so gently she fell into it, into him. There was a hard, hot rush in her middle, though her mind drifted on the crest of her emotions, like a feather floating on the stormy sea.

Quin loved the feel of his rough fingertips as they found her now. She surrendered to the sensation, growing liquid and pliant beneath his touch. A haze of desire clouded her mind but she didn't fight it. She wanted—no, needed—to let go.

His fingers coasted over one of her breasts, and his mouth followed. Deke's tongue teased her nipple, circling until it pebbled and she was arching up to meet him with a gasp. "Yes," she sighed as his hand cupped the other breast, kicking her heart rate up another notch. She brushed her hands across his back, tugging at the shirt he wore. "Off," she demanded.

Deke complied with a low chuckle and she traced the shape of him, the muscles and feathering of hair on his chest and abdomen. Even if she'd wanted to stop, she wouldn't have been able to. Why had she resisted him until this moment? Oh, yeah. Her job. Duty. But as she fell further under Deacon's spell, all her doubts had fled until she arrived at this moment. Duty, with all its demands, was only a faint echo in her mind.

His mouth demanded more from her, his hands showing her the way. She was ready, needy, breathless with desire. She wanted more, wanted him. Now. Quin tried to tell him that, but her words turned into a moan as his hand trailed across her belly, then delved deeper, slipping beneath the elastic band of her borrowed sweatpants. Quin worried, for a moment, about her unsexy clothing. Then she looked up, saw the shimmers of heat in Deacon's gaze and knew it was all for her. Because of her.

Why was he taking so long? This endless torment of

sweet touches and kisses was driving her to the brink. He finally stripped the sweats off her, leaving her exposed and vulnerable until he kissed her in the most intimate way possible. His tongue sent shivers into her core and raised goose bumps on her skin.

"Please," she begged, not knowing if she'd managed to speak the word.

His mouth and fingers sent her on a soaring spiral up and up until she couldn't breathe, until she hung suspended on the edge of something wonderful. And then she fell, her body racked with a shuddering climax, a climax much more powerful than any she'd had.

And he was there, waiting for her when she came down. Naked. Hot. Hard. And ready. They were both ready at last. He positioned his erection at her entrance and pushed in. "Yess-s-s-s," she hissed as he entered her all the way.

Deke rested his forehead against hers, panting softly. "Gotta know, baby," he groaned, his entire body tense. "Birth control?"

How could she have forgotten? She stiffened, tried to push him off.

"Shhh. It's okay."

"No—" But he was gone. He'd withdrawn, leaving her feeling empty and unsated even though she'd just experienced the most amazing climax. He sat on the edge of the bed, reaching into the drawer of his nightstand. She heard foil tearing. She watched his hands moving in his lap, and then he was back.

"I won't ever put you at risk, Quin. Never."

Something eased in her chest but he didn't move

to enter her again. "I want kids. Someday. In the right time. In the right way. With the right woman. Okay?"

She considered his words. Was he saying she was the right woman? At that moment, she wanted to be. "Okay," she whispered. And then he was inside her again.

Quin rode a hazy wave of desire, her insides still fluttering from her earlier climax. He slid in and out of her, hitting spots, changing rhythm, drawing her center tighter and tighter until she was on the brink once again. She fought letting go, clung to a shred of control until, at last, they were both there in the same moment.

Deke throbbed inside her and a throaty groan ground from between his teeth. She let go then, filled with helpless shudders. Her orgasm set her body on fire. Skyrockets burst behind her eyes and in her core. Heart. Mind. Body. All of her was joined in perfect synchronicity with the man who lay spent and panting on top of her.

How had she resisted him so long? And most important, why? He filled her with a tenderness she'd never thought herself capable of feeling. He was suddenly kissing her face, her cheeks, murmuring soft words of comfort to her. That was when she understood her skin was slick with tears.

"God, baby, did I hurt you?" He moved to roll away, and she stopped him by wrapping her legs around his waist.

"No. No. I'm fine. I'm perfect. I…" She offered a bemused laugh. "I don't know why I'm crying. I'm happy. So very happy."

And she was, inexplicably so. Quin wanted to grab this feeling, capture it somehow and place it in a treasure chest like the one where Deke kept his angel. She wanted to keep it forever. Then, whenever she was feeling sad or unhappy, she could open the chest, take out the memory and experience it all over again.

"I think I'm falling in love with you."

His words took her breath away because she wasn't sure she hadn't done the same. She didn't reply, though, her feelings too raw and unfocused.

Chuckling softly, he rolled to the side but took her with him so that she was snuggled next to him. "Progress," he said, laughter hiding behind the word.

"What do you mean?"

"You didn't hit me. And you didn't run."

Sixteen

Christmas Day dawned with skies of pink and orange as the sun peeked over the horizon. Deke was already up and puttering in the great room. He'd done some major scrounging but he'd come up with some gifts for Quin. Some were pretty cheesy but he wanted the pleasure of watching her unwrap presents. If things went right, he had one special gift for her.

The throaty growl of a diesel engine drew him to the front windows. As he watched, a yellow front-end loader crawled up the drive pushing snow out of its way. A train of vehicles followed in its wake. The cavalry had arrived. Deke didn't know whether to laugh or get upset, though it didn't matter. His idyllic interlude with Quin and Noelle had come to an end.

He headed to the bedroom to give Quin a heads-up. She was still asleep when he woke her with a kiss. "Merry Christmas, sleepyhead."

"Mmm, Merry Christmas," she said around a yawn. Her eyes narrowed. "What's that noise?"

"The cavalry. My family has arrived to celebrate."

She leaped out of bed like a scalded cat, hissing and yowling as she flew into the bathroom. "Why didn't you warn me!"

He followed her in as she jumped into the shower before the water heated. He muffled his laughter as she yowled again. "If I'd known, I would have. I did warn you that Christmas is a big deal to my family. They decided to bring it to us this year."

"How did they get here?"

"Front-end loader with a plow." She poked her head out and glowered at him, her expression suspicious. Definitely time to retreat.

As the day wore on, Deke found himself watching from the sidelines, which suited him just fine. His mother and brothers had brought presents and food. Noelle and Quin were the centers of attention, and while he considered rescuing Quin, he didn't. He was too fascinated watching the interactions.

Bridger sidled up to him at the kitchen island. "You like her." Deke hoped his expression didn't give him away. "Whoa. Seriously?" Bridger nudged him. "So it's more. She's cool, big bro." Bridge lowered his voice even further. "You know we've talked to Noelle's mom. Chance and Cash are working out the arrangements, financial and otherwise. Are you *sure* this is what you want? Taking on a baby is a huge responsibility, Deke."

"I know. I love that little girl."

"I think you love someone else, too, bro." Bridger cut his eyes to Quin.

He'd been drifting along enjoying this thing between him and Quin. He liked her. A lot. Even when she drove him crazy—and man, did she do that in all sorts of ways. Since he'd talked her into his bed, his thoughts had turned to something more. Something permanent.

Deke considered his response. He'd been headed toward this since the moment Quincy Kincaid walked into his life. "Yeah, you might be right."

Later, after the turkey and dressing, after the pumpkin pie, Deke knew the moment had arrived. He slipped into his room and pawed through a wooden box hidden on a shelf in his closet until he found the box holding the ring he'd inherited from his grandmother. Wasting no time, he walked back through the kitchen, snagged Quin's hand and urged her into the mudroom. He handed her a coat and a knit cap and pointed to the brand-new pair of snow boots she'd received for Christmas. He still didn't know how his mother had accomplished all the presents.

"If you're dragging me outside for a snowball fight…"

"Nope. Just some time alone. I love my family, but…"

He shrugged into his sheepskin rancher coat and settled his Stetson on his head. He slipped the box into his coat pocket. Deke snagged a muffler hanging on the coatrack and wrapped it around Quin's neck and checked to make sure his family had retired to the living room. He held his index finger to his mouth, took

Quin's hand and sneaked through the door leading to the expansive deck.

During the course of the day, the promise of blue skies had faded behind a layer of clouds. As Deke cleared off a spot on the wide railing circling the deck, huge, fluffy flakes began to drift down. The world was quiet and peaceful and the snow-covered fields created a soft backdrop to the vibrant woman he boosted up to sit on the rail.

"I feel like I'm in a snow globe."

"You look like it, too," Deke teased. He leaned into her and kissed a snowflake off her eyelashes. "We need to talk," he blurted.

Quin's expression turned bemused. "About what?"

"The way I feel. About you. I like you, Quin. You know that. But it's more."

"More?" Did her breath hitch?

"Yeah. More. Seeing you with my family, with Noelle. Being with you these past few days? I love you, Quin. Shhh—" He hurried to interrupt her protests. "Just let me finish. I know we haven't known each other long. I know circumstances have been…weird. But I know what I feel in my heart. You're one of a kind, Quincy Kincaid, and I want you to be mine. For now and always."

Her eyes were wide as she watched him and her throat worked as she swallowed. "What are you saying, Deke?"

"I love you, Quin. And I want to marry you. Make a family with you." He pulled the box out of his pocket and opened it.

She swallowed again and raised her eyes from the ring to meet his gaze. "Deacon?"

"Please say yes, Quin."

"Are you…are you sure about this?"

"More sure than I've ever been of anything in my life."

A hesitant smile curved the corners of her mouth, then spread all the way to her eyes. "Yes," she whispered. "Yes!" she shouted, throwing her arms around his neck.

"Yo, Deacon! You know it's not official until you go down on one knee, right?" Cooper yelled from the doorway.

Ignoring his family, Deacon slipped the ring on her finger. The ring looked antique, with a large sapphire encircled by diamonds. She stared at it, almost afraid to meet his gaze. What was she doing? This was crazy! She was nobody—a cop who got snowed in with a star. But she'd caught him looking at her, when he thought she wasn't aware of his attention. He wore the same soft expression she saw when he took care of Noelle.

He loved her. And from his family's reaction, they weren't opposed to this. She tried to make sense of things, of her emotions. Did she love him? Had she only answered "yes" because he'd surprised her? She met his eyes now, gazed deeply into them, searching for the truth of his feelings, the truth of her own.

Deacon looked…dazed. And happy. There was a tenderness in his look that came close to undoing her.

Their chemistry had been explosive from the first, and she could admit that it was mutual. And while she wavered between exasperation and affection, there'd been distrust. Was it gone now? Because any sort of long-term relationship, much less marriage, had to be based on mutual trust.

"I love you," he whispered as a smile spread across his face. "I love you!" he all but shouted, much to the amusement of his family.

Something eased in her heart and she smiled. The hopes and dreams she hadn't considered before meeting Deacon were becoming reality. This felt right, *Deacon* felt right, being here with him and Noelle, who was babbling at everyone from Katherine's arms, felt right. Six brothers and a mother-in-law. This is what Quin was getting by saying yes.

She felt a little insecure when she offered the words back, but accepted their truth. "I love you, too, Deacon."

When they came back inside, he wanted nothing more than to spend the rest of Christmas Day alone with his new fiancée. His family had other plans. As a way to torture them, he put a movie in the DVD player. The chorus of groans that accompanied the opening credits for *Love Actually* was his reward.

"Suck it up, buttercups. This movie is a Christmas present to Quin and we're watchin' it."

Halfway through the movie, every last one of them had decided they had someplace else to be. Deke paused the movie. Dillon and his mother were the last to leave. After hugs and kisses with his mom, he made turkey sandwiches and brought them on paper plates to Quin. He settled on the couch with her and sort of got into the movie.

The fire had burned down to glowing embers but it still put out enough heat for the room to be cozy. Quin snuggled deeper under the fleece blanket he'd tucked around her. They'd both dozed off during a second movie and darkness cocooned them.

He kissed her, his hands smoothing the cashmere sweater that had been a gift. Pressing another kiss to the soft skin under her jaw, he felt her pulse tripping beneath his lips.

Languidly, not fully awake, Quin rolled into him with a small sigh. She arched her hips, seeking contact with his. Deke had always worried about the roughness of his fingertips, calloused from years of playing the guitar. Conscious of that, he lightly stroked over the soft, warm flesh of her belly. He moved slowly, removing her clothes until she wore nothing but skin.

He stepped away just long enough to strip out of his own clothes and grab a condom, then climbed back onto the couch and positioned himself so she was beneath him. He brushed fingertips across her throat, slid his tongue along the seam of her lips and whispered his erotic intentions in her ear, all meant to arouse her from sleep and send her to a place where pleasure was sweet.

She said his name, then said it again after he took her mouth in a kiss meant to charm. He cupped her breast, plumped it to taste. Her breath quickened and she arched, squirming beneath him and swiveling her hips. He knew what she wanted, knew she'd be wet and ready as he slid his hand down to cup her.

Fingers stroking, teasing, he gently pinched her tender flesh, and she catapulted from that drowsy half sleep straight into urgent demand. He hardened more but Deke was determined to bring her to full desire before he sought his own release. He ran his hands over her, exploring the curves, the softness over her well-toned muscles.

Touching her made his pulse pound, sending hot blood streaking through his body. Quin reached for him with her left hand and he saw the flash of diamonds and platinum on her ring finger. He was shocked by the ferocious desire the sight built in him. His legs tangled with hers, and quiet need flared into flagrant want.

In this moment, there was only sensation. Her mouth searched for his, and their lips met. Her hands clutched at his shoulders. They were in sync—moods, needs and desires matching. They both wanted more. He would give all that she wanted and he would take all that he could. He was greedy.

Awake now, she watched him sheath himself through half-lidded eyes. She lifted her knees, spreading wider for him, then locked her ankles across the small of his back. Bracing on one hand, he teased her entrance but she took him by surprise, surging up to take him in. He sank to the hilt in her wet, welcoming heat. Dang, but he loved this woman.

Quin gasped when he withdrew and as he pushed back in, she shuddered, already coming. He choked, his breath clogging his lungs as his heart thundered. He rode out her orgasm with gritted teeth. He tried to tell her how he felt, how much she meant to him, but words refused to come. She tightened her legs, drew him deeper inside her.

He had to hold on, had to make this last, make it perfect for her. Deke pulled out, amid her protests. He spent endless time arousing her again. With his fingers, his mouth, he teased and tantalized. Her body fascinated him. Curvy yet sleek, it filled him with joy. Her skin quivered where he touched her and his own reacted in kind.

"Again, darlin'."

"No, I can't," she panted.

To prove she could, he slid his fingers into her. Her short nails sank into the skin of his back and he bet tomorrow he'd have half-moon marks as evidence of her loss of control. Her breath gasped out in short puffs and her hips pumped against his hand.

Her wet heat seduced him and he wanted to bury himself again. One more moment and he would indulge himself. "Just let go, Quin."

Saying her name was like a magic word. She shuddered, cried out and hung on to him. He loved watching her face when she climaxed, the way her mouth opened, her lips wet from quick licks of her tongue. The way her eyes flew open then went half-lidded, her gaze warm and sensual. He didn't let up, urging her with his fingers to ride the crest of sensation while he watched. She quivered, her breath seemingly locked in her lungs, and he sent her over the edge again, then let her melt against him as he eased her back to earth.

Caught up in her pleasure, he let passion and love guide him now. She pulled him on top and her hand fisted around him, guiding him to the silken heat of her body. He slid inside and then found her mouth. She kissed him, and he forgot everything. There was nothing but the two of them.

Goose bumps danced across her skin with every brush of his lips. After three orgasms, Deke was almost surprised at her responses. She met each stroke, swiveling her hips and driving him deep inside. He took her hands, laced their fingers and pumped his hips. Faster. And she rose to meet him, skin flushed, breath catching, eyelashes fluttering. He grinned, neck muscles tensing as white-hot sensation built at the base of his spine, spilling out into him. He was going to make her soar again.

Her fingers squeezed his. "Deacon."

Just as calling her name had set her off earlier, a switch tripped inside him and his control broke. He surged against her and she met him, held him, as he shuddered and throbbed deep inside her. *Hold on*, he thought. He had to hold on because he was spinning off and he wasn't going without Quin. She held him back, clinging as they slid down into the quiet. He rested his head between her breasts, eyes closed.

Right here. Right now. Just like this. This was what life was supposed to be.

Later, she lay with her head on his chest, their legs entwined. Drowsy, he listened to the easy sound of her breathing and the crackle of the fire. His ring glistened on her hand. He kissed her temple and whispered, "Merry Christmas, darlin'."

Seventeen

Self-conscious about the glittering ring on her left hand, Quin kept her hands shoved in her pockets while riding in the wrecker back to the OHP garage. Deke, his foreman and others had dug her patrol car out of the snow just in time for the wrecker to pull it back onto the roadway. It wasn't drivable and she dreaded the paperwork she faced.

Quin walked through the door to OHP headquarters with a grin stretching her cheeks. She'd stared at Deke's ring on her finger while opening the door and she was positively giddy. Deacon Tate had asked her to marry him. And she'd said yes! She did a series of little dance steps as she headed toward the requisitions office.

The secretary noticed, which wasn't surprising.

Quin figured her happiness was flashing like a neon sign in Vegas. Unable to resist, Quin showed her the ring and explained she'd gotten engaged for Christmas.

"That's so romantic," the woman said, gushing. "Who's the lucky man? Anyone we know?"

And that cooled Quin's jets. The media, already dogging Deacon, would latch on to this latest event and worry it like a meaty bone. Besides, the whole idea of marrying him was still new enough, still nerve-racking enough, that she wanted to keep Deke's identity a secret for a little while longer.

"No, probably not. He's not in law enforcement."

"Smart." The secretary handed over a pile of papers and pointed to an empty desk. "Have fun."

Quin laughed and after silencing her phone, set to work filling in the blanks that would lead her to getting a new patrol car.

Once she was done and waiting for one to be assigned, Dispatch contacted her and instructed her to appear at the main offices of Child Protective Services as soon as possible.

Thirty minutes later, she walked into a room at the Department of Human Services and wondered if she was facing a board of inquiry. Two women and a man sat on the far side of a conference table. There was one lone chair on her side. She slid into it and braced herself.

"It has come to our attention, Trooper Kincaid, that you've spent the last week living with Deacon Tate." The younger of the two women, who'd been assigned as Noelle's caseworker, opened the discussion.

Quin straightened in her chair, hoping she didn't blush. "That's correct. I was at his home making a welfare check when the blizzard hit. I've just now returned to duty, though I'm technically on vacation. Why?"

"What did you observe while you were there?" the man asked.

"Observe?" Quin already didn't like the tone of his meeting.

"How did Mr. Tate react to your presence?" the older woman snapped.

Quin considered her words carefully, then answered, "Mr. Tate was very hospitable."

"I'm sure he was," the woman replied archly before conferring in whispers with her colleagues, all three of them glancing at her surreptitiously.

"Certain information has come to us," the caseworker finally said.

Just over an hour later, Quin stumbled out of the office. She hadn't believed them at first. The man they described wasn't the Deacon she'd come to know. She wasn't a foolish woman. She was a cop. A trained investigator. And she hadn't gone into this situation with stars in her eyes like some silly groupie. They had evidence, though.

According to information CPS had discovered, Deacon Tate, Mr. All-American Nice Guy, was a publicist's fabrication. He was considered difficult to work with and in need of further "humanizing." Quin read the reports, incredulous at first, then disbelieving. The tipping point was a memo from a senior record executive.

What better story to put out than Deacon Tate, the

country boy with the heart of gold, had taken in an abandoned baby…and romanced the cop assigned to the case. It could be a women's cable network movie. Rich singer falls in love with baby and poor cop, he asks the cop to marry him, they adopt the baby and all live happily ever after.

The older woman's eyes had held pity as she explained the situation.

Bottom line? Deacon had offered Noelle's mother 25,000 dollars to buy the baby. Despite all the evidence, Quin hadn't believed it. Not at first. Not until they brought in Noelle's mother. Amanda confirmed that she'd received the money to sign private adoption papers, and that someone with the Barron law firm had taken her to a bank to set up an account.

CPS wanted Quin to testify against Deke. All her previous reservations came flooding back. He was a performer, right? She'd watched his music videos, even commented on how real he seemed acting out the songs' stories. She thought back, reviewed all the things she and Deke had done together. Had he just been pretending with her?

Quin should have known her engagement was too good to be true. Should have known a man like Deacon would never love someone like her, that his family would never take in a stranger. It was all some publicity stunt. Using a baby as a pawn was despicable. She knew that from firsthand experience. Her parents, that rich couple—they'd all played that game using her and her brothers. She twisted the ring off her finger and shoved it in the pocket of her uniform pants.

* * *

Deke sat at the kitchen island, one hip hitched on a stool, his music composition book spread out on the granite counter. Noelle was asleep in her playpen so he strummed his acoustic guitar softly, pausing to jot notes and words, though he was mostly distracted by other thoughts.

After he'd helped dig out Quin's police car yesterday morning, he'd gone into Oklahoma City with the baby for an appointment of his own. Chance had set up a meeting with Noelle's mother.

"Why?" he'd asked her. "Why accuse me of being Noelle's father?"

Amanda—Mandy, she'd asked to be called—had cried and apologized. "Your music, it always makes me feel special, Mr. Deacon, like you're singing straight to my heart. When Noelle's daddy took off, I didn't know what t'do. I don't got no family t'speak of. And you have such a big one. I'd gotten a ride to the casino thinkin' I might be able to get a job. I saw your bus sittin' there and I just…" The girl hung her head and wiped her tears with the handkerchief Chance handed her. "I just got to thinkin' what it would be like if you were Noelle's daddy, about what a wonderful life she'd have. I knew you'd love her. I didn't mean t'cause trouble for you."

Deke's heart had gone out to the girl and he'd decided to help her. She'd been so relieved and excited when he offered her what amounted to a scholarship—tuition and living expenses while she attended cosmetology school. He'd tried to call Quin on the way home, to tell her what he planned to do. In the end, he couldn't be truly upset with Mandy. She only wanted a better life for her daughter. Besides, he would have never met Quin.

Even coming back to a house with no Quin, he'd had Noelle, so the place didn't feel empty, as it once had. His life was becoming everything he hoped for. He'd found a woman he loved, a baby they'd raise together. Family. He would have a ready-made family.

Before she'd left yesterday morning, Quin had decided to stay in town. He didn't like sleeping alone. He missed her sweet, sleepy-eyed kisses first thing in the morning. He'd tried calling her several times yesterday, last night and this morning, but his calls rolled to voice mail and his texts when unanswered. Quin was a state trooper—an important job. She'd been out of pocket for a week and probably had lots of work to catch up on—even though she was supposed to be on vacation. But they were engaged and he thought she'd return his call when she found a moment.

Something dark suddenly crawled through him, a worry he couldn't quite shake. What if she'd accepted his proposal because she didn't want to hurt his feelings? What if she was ducking his calls because she didn't know how to break it to him—that she didn't love him and wanted to break up? No, that couldn't be why.

He thought back to what they'd done, what he'd said after the proposal. He'd told her over and over that he loved her. She'd said the same, out there on the deck with his family watching. But later, had Quin said the words again? Doubts wormed their way in despite his efforts to squash them. As a result, here he sat, at 10:30 a.m., fidgeting and full of nervous energy. He couldn't wait to see her again and was surprised at how much he missed her. After being stuck together 24/7 for a week, he was used to having her here. She'd left on Tuesday, it was only Wednesday, yet every time he looked up, Deke expected to see her on the couch reading or watching TV. And every time, the room was empty.

Someone knocked on the door, and his heart leaped. He wasn't expecting any family so it had to be Quin. But why didn't she just walk in? She knew he didn't lock the door when he was home. They were engaged, and this would be her home, too. She didn't need to knock.

He set the guitar on the island and jogged to the door. He threw it open, a welcoming smile on his face. Two strangers stood there—a woman bundled up in a puffy coat, looking pinch-faced and angry. A burly, gruff-faced Oklahoma County deputy stood next to her, and he spoke before Deke could.

"Deacon Tate?"

"Yes?"

The deputy shoved a piece of paper at him as the woman barged past, striding into his home. "Where's the baby?" she demanded.

"The baby? What's going on?"

"Read the order," the deputy said.

He did and shoved a hand in his hip pocket. The

deputy stiffened and ordered, "Hands where I can see them."

Deke held his hands out to his sides. "I was just reaching for my phone, deputy."

"Don't make any sudden moves, *sir*. I have no way of knowing what you're reaching for."

The man's emphasis on the honorific wasn't lost on Deke so he didn't bother arguing or asking the obvious question because yes, the deputy knew who he was. From his position he watched the woman grab up the baby, but when Noelle started crying, he tensed.

"What are you doing to her?" he yelled.

"It's no longer your concern," the woman barked as she returned holding the upset baby.

"At least get her travel blanket from her room. You can't take her out in this cold dressed only in her onesie!"

After a minute of hesitation, the woman acquiesced. "Fine. He can show us."

The deputy shadowed him across the great room, the woman following. Deke stopped at the nursery door and caught the look of surprise on the social worker's face when she stepped inside. What had she been expecting? That he stuffed Noelle into a cardboard box to sleep? He pointed with his chin to the tall dresser. "Second drawer. There's a Pendleton travel blanket thing that works with her carrier and car seat."

"I have a car seat."

"Yeah, I just bet." The one installed in his truck was top-of-the-line and had the highest safety rating. He could just imagine what she had in her state car. They allowed him to retrieve the blanket, then they returned to the front door.

Deacon battled to stay calm, especially when the woman swept out of his house without allowing him to kiss the baby goodbye. Adding insult, the deputy waited until the woman's car disappeared.

"Word of advice," the man called as he got into his patrol car. "Don't follow."

Seriously? Did they truly believe he'd go tearing after the woman and kidnap the baby or something? Why would he do something that stupid when he had something far more powerful in his corner—his family.

What he didn't understand was what had triggered this removal. It wasn't until he was reading the order to Chance over the phone that realization crashed into him. Quin. She'd known about the order. That was why she hadn't returned his calls. Her name was listed as a witness for the state. *Given the current guardian's unusual attachment to the child, it is this officer's opinion that he will not willingly release the child to her natural parent.*

What the hell? Yes, he loved Noelle but if her mother truly wanted her back and was able to take care of her, he'd do everything he could to help.

"Deacon?" Chance sounded cautious. "I thought you and Quin were engaged."

"Yeah, me, too. I… What's going on, Chance? Why would they take Noelle like this?" But what he really wanted to know was why Quin would do this to him… to Noelle.

"I don't know. They used a juvenile court judge. I

put in a call to Judge Nelligan. We'll get to the bottom of things. In the meantime, hang tight and find out what Quin knows."

Yeah, he'd like to do that but she would have to answer her damn phone for that to happen. After a long pause, he admitted, "She's not taking my calls, Chance."

Silence stretched over the phone line. "Aw, hell, Deke," Chance finally said. "Is it possible she set you up?"

Was he that big of an idiot, his family all fools to believe her? He didn't know if she was capable of doing this, if she was that cold. But why else would she have given testimony to take Noelle away from him? Quin's apparent betrayal ripped his heart out of his chest. A knife twisting in his gut would have been more humane. The damn woman had shared his bed, accepted his marriage proposal. Even now she wore his grandmother's ring. Well, not for long if she was playing him.

"I honestly don't know, Chance. I… Dammit, I love her. I thought she loved me. At least that's what she said."

"I'll find out what's going on, Deke. We'll get Noelle back. I promise."

Quin felt queasy. The low-level headache she'd been fighting since finding out about Deacon yesterday roared back to life as soon as she entered Troop A headquarters. A few of her colleagues were there— some finishing up reports before going off duty, others checking in prior to hitting the road for their shift. Now that her part in the baby Noelle investigation was over, she could get back to patrolling Oklahoma's highways. She blew off the remainder of her vacation. She was desperate to stay busy so she didn't have time to think.

She hadn't slept well last night. Oh, who was she kidding? She hadn't slept at all.

Quin had done the right thing so it couldn't be guilt keeping her awake. She'd been an idiot to trust a sexy man who knew how to push every last one of her buttons. She had a duty to protect the innocent and what Deke had done was inexcusable. Deacon Tate as a single father? Ridiculous. As evidenced by his insane declaration that he loved her and wanted to make a family with her and that baby. They didn't know each other well enough to be in love—the week spent snowed in notwithstanding. And she should have known he was playing her.

Removing Noelle from Deacon's custody was the right decision. Amanda wasn't exactly in a place to take care of her child. But she'd told them she wanted to go to school. Get her own place to live. Find a job. Based on that, the CPS caseworker had drawn up a plan—one that included parenting classes. It wouldn't be easy but little Noelle would be safe with a foster family until Mandy got her life together. Quin hoped the girl would. Then the little family would be reunited and everything would be fine.

And Quin wouldn't have to deal with Deacon Tate. Because she'd been out of her mind to fall for his seduction. Granted, he was the sexiest man she'd ever been around—much less kissed and made love with.

The man was...*gifted* in that department. Her cheeks warmed with the thought of what they'd done, but he was still a jerk. She had to remember that. He'd taken advantage of a naive girl. Quin didn't want to admit that she'd allowed him to take advantage of her, as well.

"Yo, Kincaid!" Fingers snapped in front of her face and she blinked, realizing she'd totally blanked out.

"What?" She glared at the smirking trooper standing in front of her.

"Whoa, Quin. You're the one with the thousand-yard stare. I called your name five times. Lieutenant Charles wants you."

"Oh, thanks." She headed to her supervisor's office as the other cop called after her.

"You should think about maybe getting more sleep. You look like something my wife's cat dragged in." He laughed and walked away before she could think of a retort.

Sadly, he was right. She did need more sleep. And obviously, her attempt at applying makeup that morning hadn't concealed her restless nights. Quin braced herself, her stomach twisting in knots at the thought of what faced her. She was pretty sure the entire coalition of the Barrons' and Tates' powerful friends was about to dump on her.

The lieutenant was in the break room pouring a cup of coffee and he looked up as she paused in the doorway. He preempted her question. "You have a visitor. Interview room A. You need to fix this, Kincaid." He turned back to his coffee, dismissing her.

Great. She'd done the right thing, and now it was

all coming back on her. Well, fine. Just fine. She'd go deal with whatever minion Deacon had sent. She'd set that person straight. Then she'd get back to doing her job. Full of righteous indignation, she stalked down the hallway.

When she reached the interview room, Quin didn't knock. She barged through the door. The person sitting there jerked liked she'd been punched, one hand pressed to her chest as she jumped to her feet. Quin halted two steps inside the room as she recognized her visitor. Mandy Brooks was the last person she expected to see. The girl's eyes looked bruised from exhaustion and her posture indicated she was ready to bolt.

Quin studied her. In a nervous gesture, Mandy tucked a lank strand of hair behind her ear with trembling fingers. The kid looked beaten down by life and Quin didn't like the resigned expression etched on the girl's face.

She gentled her voice. "Hey, Mandy. I wasn't expecting you. Here, sit down."

"I'm sorry, ma'am. I didn't... You..." The girl inhaled, working to control the shaking in her hands. "I'm sorry. You scared me bustin' in like that and all."

Approaching carefully, Quin hitched one hip on the metal table, keeping a little distance between them. "My fault, Mandy. I was expecting someone else."

"I...don't mean t'take up your time or nothin'. I know you're really busy but...I just had t'talk to you."

Quin resisted the urge to rub her temples. She needed to tread lightly here and the headache was making it hard to concentrate. "It's okay, hon. What do you need to talk about?"

Amanda twisted her fingers into knots, then spread them to smooth down the worn denim covering her thighs. "I gotta say this, ma'am."

"You can call me Quincy, Mandy."

"Yes, ma'am. I mean, Quin…cy. It's like this, you see. I know you think you're helpin' and all but you're ruinin' everything." The girl's words ran together at the end, her tone no longer hesitant.

Quin did her best to decipher what the girl was implying. She gave up because she had no idea where Mandy was headed. "I don't understand…"

"Of course you don't. You're strong, Miz Quincy. Strong and brave. Not like me. I'm not those things. Never will be. And see, that's what I gotta make you understand. What those people at CPS are doin'? Trying to keep Noelle from Mr. Deke? That's just wrong."

Warmth suffused her cheeks as Quin attempted to curb her temper. "Did he send you here?" It would be just like the sorry son of a gun to send this poor girl in an attempt to sway her.

"No! How could you even think that?"

The shocked indignation on Mandy's face, followed quickly by fear, made Quin realize she sounded far harsher than she'd intended. She breathed through her anger, worked to school her expression into something softer, something more sympathetic. How could she be upset with Mandy? The girl had a huge crush on Deacon. Of course she would be protective of him. After all, Mandy had entrusted the man with her baby.

"It's not like that at all, Miz Quincy. I—" Mandy snapped her mouth shut and swallowed before continuing. "I haven't seen Mr. Deke since y'all took my little Noelle away from him. An' see? That's why I'm here. What y'all did, it's just wrong."

So much for soft and sympathetic. Before Quin could respond, the shy, reticent girl she was familiar with dissolved right in front of her, and in the girl's place stood a momma bear.

"How could you, Miz Quincy? You say you're my friend but you go behind my back and you... Lordy. You hurt him so bad. You hurt my baby girl. And you just keep on hurtin' folks for no reason."

Quin needed to regain control of this situation. "That's not true, Mandy. We're doing what is best for you and Noelle."

"No, you ain't!" Agitated, Mandy surged to her feet and paced the confines of the interview room. "I thought you understood. But you don't. You're just like all those people at Child Services."

"Mandy, please..." Quin kept her voice calm.

"No. You don't get it. Not at all. I'm broken and I always will be. The system broke me. And now you want to throw my baby in there to get chewed up."

"You aren't broken—"

"The devil I ain't! I'll always be broken. I'm not like you. You're strong. I'm not. And I won't ever be. No child deserves a momma who can't face the world and protect 'em. And I can't. That's why I gave her to Mr. Deacon. I knew he'd take care of her. Knew he'd love her. And he does. He brought her to see me so I could decide what t'do. He loves her with his whole heart. I see it every time he looks at her, every time he says her name."

Mandy brushed at her cheeks and cleared her throat. Quin was too stunned to speak.

"And you know what, Miz Quincy? He told me all about you. How he loved you, and how y'all were gonna make a family with Noelle. When he said your name, when he talked about the future an' you? He looked that same way. I'd give anything to have a man look like that when he thinks about me. Maybe you don't feel the same about him. That's on you, but don't take my baby away from that man—from the family that loves her and will take care of her for the rest of her life."

Tears flowed unheeded down Mandy's cheeks, her body racked with silent sobs. Quin was at a complete loss as to what to do. She wanted to comfort the girl but Mandy stood there encased in misery, arms around herself as if to contain the storm raging within her.

The door banged open, slamming against the wall. Both women whirled. Deacon stood there with Chance Barron, and two troopers. Part of Quin's brain recorded the difference between Mandy's reaction and her own. Mandy slumped in relief—like Deacon had just ridden in on his white horse to rescue her. Quin, on the other hand, felt detached from the scene, as Mandy's words trickled through her brain.

He loves her with his whole heart. I see it every time he looks at her, every time he says her name.

When he said your name, when he talked about the future an' you? He looked that same way.

Only he wasn't looking at her with love. Not at the moment. She'd always thought Deacon was easygoing. Boy, had she been wrong. The man standing there breathing hard looked like he *could* slay dragons.

One of the troopers cleared his throat and jerked his thumb in Chance's direction. "This guy says he's the girl's lawyer. And this one…" He gave Deke an assessing look. "He claims to be your fiancé. You need us to stay, Quin?"

"No. I'll handle this, Rizzo. Thanks." The troopers exited, shutting the door behind them.

"What did you do to her?" Deacon's voice fairly vibrated with anger.

That got her back up. "Me? Not a darn thing. What nonsense have you been telling her?"

"Nonsense? Oh, you mean like I love her little girl and want to adopt Noelle? Like I want to make sure Mandy gets her education and gets a chance to live a real life? Like I care about what happens to her and to Noelle? Like I loved you?"

"Don't fight," Mandy pleaded. "Don't fight because of me."

Deacon strode to the girl. He touched Mandy's shoulder, his hand and expression gentle. Jealousy stabbed through Quin, hot and fast like a bullet. She glowered at the pair through narrowed eyes until her cop training took over. She slowly regained control. Focused. And really looked at them.

That was when she realized there was nothing sexual in the way Deacon touched Mandy. His hold was careful, comforting, like a father's, or a big brother's.

"Go outside with Chance, Mandy," Deacon directed. "It'll be okay. We'll get this mess untangled. I'll fix it. You just have to trust me." He turned the girl over to Chance, nodded at some question in his cousin's eyes and waited until the door was closed behind them before he faced Quin.

Trust. That was what it boiled down to. Quin understood now. Mandy *did* know Deacon better than she did. He wasn't doing any of this for publicity, for recognition, despite evidence to the contrary—evidence she now suspected had been fabricated. He was doing it because he really was a good guy. A man so good he'd taken in an abandoned baby because it was the right thing to do. And then he fell in love with that baby and wanted to give her a home. He'd fallen in love with the cop who fought him every step, and wanted to make a home with her, too. Quin had hurt him deeply because, she realized too late, he had truly loved her. And she hadn't trusted him—or herself—enough to believe.

She turned away and pulled her cell phone from her hip pocket. Quin didn't understand why the numbers were blurry as she attempted to dial the social worker who'd removed Noelle. She felt Deke's glare knifing into her back.

"You callin' for backup now, Trooper Kincaid? Don't bother. I'm leaving. You don't have to worry about seein' me ever again. Since you're not wearing it, you can deliver my grandmother's ring to Chance when you see him in court. We're done."

Quin's call to Child Services went to voice mail. She hung up. Her denial was on her lips as she turned to face Deke. Only the room was empty. He'd gone. She was left standing alone. Frustrated, she considered chasing him down so she could explain. That was when the truth hit.

She'd blown it as far as Deacon was concerned. He'd loved her. Loved her enough he'd wanted to spend the rest of his life with her. She'd been waiting for the other shoe to drop, quick to assign motives where there'd been none. Wrapping her arms around her waist, she bent over, sick to her stomach. She'd ruined the best thing to ever happen to her. Quin had destroyed any chance they might have had by her actions. Because she hadn't trusted Deacon, had believed the worst of him before hearing his side.

Tears streamed unheeded down her cheeks as she sank onto the metal chair. She felt numb, which was a blessing. When the pain finally came, she knew it would eviscerate her.

Eighteen

The last thing Deke wanted to do was sing in front of a crowd of strangers, but Chase had set up this appearance months ago when he was wrangling something out of the city fathers. Under normal circumstances, this appearance would be a piece of cake. But a hard-nosed cop had ripped his heart out and then stomped on it.

And God help him but he still loved her.

The boys continued to walk on eggshells around him. They'd come out to the ranch to work on some of the new songs for the next album. Yeah, the new stuff was maudlin as hell, and Dillon had been quick to ask what Deke had done to screw things up with Quin. Only he hadn't done a thing. Not a blasted thing.

He'd taken in an abandoned baby. He'd fallen in

love with her. And he'd fallen in love with the stubborn woman assigned to the investigation. He'd given his heart to both, wanting to adopt Noelle and help her mother, and wanting to marry Quin. Who then betrayed him and took that baby away.

The rest of the band was in the front of the bus kicking back. Deke hid in the bedroom. He didn't want to do this gig. He wanted to go home. Alone. Yeah, he might pour a tumbler full of good Kentucky whiskey and write stupid songs about broken hearts that no one but him would ever hear, but he was entitled. He'd face the rest of his life tomorrow. Tonight, he just wanted to wallow in his misery.

Deke could hear the other guys out in the living area and he had to roll his eyes. They were playing rock-paper-scissors. The loser had to come get him. He considered saving them the angst, then decided *naw*. Make them work for it. He put away the acoustic guitar. He wouldn't be strumming it tonight. Those broken-heart ballads had no place on a New Year's Eve playlist, though a few love songs were necessary. As much as he hated the thought of singing one given the sorry state of his own life, he knew their fans would be in a romantic mood.

Quin knew what she had to do. The problem was, she had no plan. And not much time to come up with one, much less execute it. She was in uniform and on crowd control, along with half of Troop A. The other half was out on the streets on drunk patrol. The night was cold but not frigid. The indoor venues were doing bang-up business. Deke and the Sons of Nashville were scheduled to take the outdoor stage in Bicentennial Park at 10:00 p.m. for a concert that ended just before midnight, when they'd lead the crowd in counting down to the New Year as the lighted ball climbed its anchor pole.

Her timing would have to be impeccable. If she distracted him during the concert—made him even angrier than he already was—he or Chance would file a complaint against her. And if she approached him before the concert…yeah, he'd just ignore her like he'd been doing since he'd walked out of the interview room.

For two hours, she patrolled the downtown area, which was roped off for Opening Night, Oklahoma City's big New Year's Eve celebration. Even with the cold temperatures, the crowd was bigger than normal— thanks to Deacon Tate and the Sons of Nashville. Free concert? Oh, heck yeah! Their fans were all over that.

From nine to ten, she fretted and answered minor calls. A public drunk. A child who fell and cut her chin. A couple fighting over flirting with the opposite sex. She was also aware of the crowd gathering around the finale stage in the park. People came out of the Norick Downtown Library, out of the Oklahoma City Museum of Art and streamed from the art deco doors of the Civic Center.

The food trucks lined up at the edge of the outdoor venue had been doing a brisk business but now they were all but deserted. The stage was set up in front of city hall. The streets surrounding the venue had been closed to vehicular traffic and already the park area between the Civic Center and city hall was wall-to-wall people. She had to figure out something before Deke's concert began.

A soft rap on the door indicated the time to mope had come to an end. "Go away," Deke yelled.

"Having trouble hearing, bro," Kenji said as he entered. "You said 'C'mon in,' right?"

Deke had to work to hide his grin. Not only were the members of his band incredible musicians, but they were also the best kind of friends. "Yeah, something like that."

"You know the girl's not worth it, right, dude?" Kenji asked in his signature Tennessee accent. "And you know there's been a million songs written about this situation, right?"

To prove his point, Kenji burst into a slightly off-key rendition of Cole Swindell's "Ain't Worth the Whiskey." The rest of the band joined in from the front of the bus.

"We are so adding that to the list tonight," Dillon yelled.

Deke considered Kenji's words. Maybe he'd rushed things with Quin. Maybe he'd suffered a bruised ego at her hands, not a broken heart. Yeah, right. Asking her to marry him had not been a spur-of-the-moment decision. The idea had been fermenting in his mind almost from the moment he first laid eyes on her. Not that he believed in love at first sight but…yeah, he believed in love at first sight when it came to Quincy

Kincaid. But loving her and forgiving her were two different animals.

Twenty minutes later, they were on stage, waiting to be introduced by the mayor of Oklahoma City. The crowd was estimated at close to 100,000. The night felt electric, energy pouring from the people spread out between city hall and the Civic Center.

Deke closed his eyes, focused. He would feed off the intensity of the audience, absorb their excitement. He lived for this. Loved it down to his very soul. Tonight, he would sing for them. And with luck, their energy would fill up the empty places in his heart.

As the mayor wrapped up the intro, Kenji started a pounding beat on his drums. Ozzie matched it with his bass guitar line. When the crowd erupted, spotlights lit the stage. The beat continued until things quieted down. A few measures later, Xander added a riff on the banjo, which Bryce followed, dueling banjos–style, with the same riff on his guitar. Dillon added the song line on his keyboard. And then Deke stepped front and center, launching into "Red Dirt Cowgirl," which he'd written for Chance and Cassidy when they got married.

The clock ticked toward midnight but as often happened when he was on stage, Deke lost himself in the music, in the crowd, in the sheer electricity shooting through the air. Until he looked down. And saw her.

Working along the outside edges of the crowd, Quin was drawn inexorably toward the stage. Like a moth to a flame. A bee to honey. Ants to a picnic. She was a walking cliché. Reaching the corner of the stage, she was no closer to forming a plan.

Time was running out. She needed to do something. And fast. The girls lined up in front of the stage caught Quin's eye. They all had big signs with printed messages on cardboard. And just like that, a plan popped into her head.

"Can I borrow your sign?" she asked the girl nearest her, all but yelling over the music blaring from nearby speakers.

The girl's eyes widened. "I recognize you! You're Deacon's Christmas cop. The one he fell in love with."

Wait. What? How could people know about her, about Deacon? Then it occurred to her—the press releases from the record-company PR department, and the statement from some executive the CPS people had shown her. She wondered if Deke knew they were still linked, and if he'd care.

"Yes," Quin said. "I need your sign, okay?"

The girl held out the piece of cardboard. "What'cha gonna do with it?"

"Try to hold on to the best thing that ever happened to me!" Quin grabbed the black Sharpie pen she habitually shoved in her hip pocket to mark evidence and scribbled on the cardboard. She waited until Deke looked her direction and then she hoisted the sign high over her head.

I'm Sorry!!!!

He stared right through her, his face blank. She

needed another sign. Quin looked around but her new friend was already on the case. The girl passed over another piece of cardboard and Quin scribbled.

When Deke glanced her way, she was ready.

I Was Wrong. All Along.

He turned his back to the audience to do a riff with Dillon on the keyboard, which gave her time to gather more signs and scribble furiously. When he faced the crowd again, she moved to stand directly in front of him, her new girl posse hard on her heels.

I Didn't Give You A Chance To Explain. Did I Mention I'm Sorry?

He still ignored her.

I Fixed It.

That got a narrowing of his eyes.

Noelle Will Be Home With You Tomorrow!

Did he just miss a chord? He was still singing but he'd stopped playing and his eyes bored into hers. She broke eye contact when she dipped her chin to write the next set of signs.

Before I Get Out Of Your Life For Good...
I Just Want You To Know...

I Love You

Deke continued crooning the words of the love song into the microphone, seemingly unmoved. She supposed that was her answer. This whole crazy, spur-of-the-moment deal had been a last-ditch effort. She offered him a smile that felt small, tentative and very, *very* sad—which was exactly how she felt.

Quin handed the signs back to the girl and yelled above the noise, "Thanks anyway. It was worth a shot."

Turning her back, she merged into the crowd and worked her way toward the street. The song ended to applause, whistles and shouts of approval. The microphone squealed from feedback and Deke's voice surrounded her.

"Somebody stop that state trooper."

A solid wall of bodies formed between her and escape. She stopped. Quin could have bulled her way through but there was something in Deke's voice that made her swivel around to face him instead.

"Come here," he ordered. Her heart skipped a beat as she moved purposely toward the stage. He gestured for her to come around to the side, then announced that Dillon was singing the next song—much to his little brother's surprise.

Deke pointed out some steps and waved for her to come up on stage. When she reached him, he pulled her out of sight of the crowd and asked, "Did you mean it?" She nodded. "I'll have Noelle back tomorrow? For New Year's Day?"

"Yes. I talked to the juvenile judge. She's rescinding her order, reinstating your custody order." She scrubbed her face with the heels of her hands. "I was so wrong, Deke. About you, about everything. CPS had all this evidence. I believed it because… I don't know why. I should have called you, let you tell me your side. Something inside me just…couldn't believe that you truly loved me. I'm so sorry. About everything."

Deke didn't say a word, simply stared at her as the music curtained them from the world. After too many stuttering heartbeats to count, he asked, "Do you love me?"

Quin had to blink rapidly as her eyes filled with tears. "With all my heart. Noelle, too."

Once again, he remained silent and when he spoke, it wasn't the words she wanted to hear. "I have to finish the show."

She nodded, mute, as she turned to the stairs and descended. She'd given it her best shot. Maybe someday, he'd forgive her.

Deke slipped his phone from his hip pocket and with frantic fingers, texted Chance. He asked about Noelle's status, filling in his cousin on what Quin had said. His phone rang and he ducked behind the speakers, hoping he could hear Chance.

"Stand by, Deke. I'm checking my messages. Tell me exactly what Quin said."

He repeated her words, his chest so tight with compressed emotion he could barely get them out.

"I'm not that familiar with the juvie judges. I know Nelligan was about to get into a jurisdiction fight with her. I had one of my investigators looking into the situation so we'd have ammunition at the emergency hearing Nelligan set. All the evidence was generated through CPS. Quin was just a witness. Aha! Found it. The clerk emailed me. We can pick Noelle up at the foster home anytime after ten tomorrow. Congrats, Deke! You're gonna be a dad after all."

Air whooshed out of his lungs and he realized the crowd was cheering. Dillon's song was over. Without stopping to think things through, Deke walked over, removed his mic from its stand and walked to the front of the stage. He searched the crowd for Quin's face, found her standing in shadows off to one side. He launched into the next song on the playlist but kept his eyes glued to Quin.

She stood frozen, her eyes on him. Almost as if she was in a trance, she began to walk back toward the stage. People noticed he was staring, turned to look. A gaggle of female fans squealed and rushed to Quin, escorting her back toward the stage. People stepped aside so there was a clear path to where he was standing.

Quin told her feet to stop walking but they paid her no mind. She was six feet away from the stage when Deke finished his song to thunderous applause. As it died down, he spoke.

"You know it's not official until I get down on one knee, right?" And he did. He dropped down, right there on the stage in front of the whole crowd. "I love you, Quincy Kincaid. Will you marry me?"

"Yes," she said. Or thought she did. No sound came

out of her mouth. But Deke must have read her lips because he was off the stage and she was flying toward him. He caught her midleap and swung her around, his lips finding hers with unerring accuracy. She'd missed his kisses, missed the hot, hungry taking of her mouth. Missed the way her heart skipped beats until it was perfectly synchronized with his.

He broke the kiss and murmured against her ear, "I love you, Quincy." He continued saying the words as he peppered her face, neck and shoulders with kisses.

Quin laughed. She couldn't help herself. Here she was in full uniform in the middle of a New Year's Eve concert, her arms and legs around the sexiest country music star in the whole world. "I love you, too," she answered each time he said it.

Then they were moving toward the stage. Deke loosened his hold on her long enough for Bryce and Xander to lift her up by her hands. Deke hopped up beside her. He swept her into his arms and kissed her again. While she was still lost in the kiss, the band started playing and the next thing she knew, Deke had her tucked up against his side. The mic was back in his hand and he was singing.

"I've been on the road for all my life. Knocking around with the boys. Never thought I'd settle down, much less with a wife."

Kenji played a sting on the drums—the sound often accompanying a lame joke—and Quin laughed as Deke didn't miss a beat.

"I'm headin' home. I'm comin' back to you. Back where I belong. Been on the road way beyond too long, an' I've been dreamin' 'bout you."

Deke cupped her cheek in the palm of his hand and gazed into her eyes as he continued singing. "My heart knew things would never be the same, the moment you walked through the door. My roamin' days are over, since you're gonna take my name.

"I'm headin' home." He launched into the chorus and the crowd sang along. Then they all got quiet—even the music went soft as Deke sang, "I need to get back to you, to the place I belong. 'Cause you hold my heart right there in your hand. I'm gonna love you for all my life, 'cause you make me a better man. Hang on girl, I'll be there soon. 'Cause I'm headin' home, I'm comin' back to you."

In that moment, standing there in Deke's arms in front of a huge crowd, she realized what she'd been missing her whole life. That sense of belonging, of *home*, and with this man, this wild, wonderful, sexy man with a voice that charmed the panties off his fans, she'd found what she'd been missing.

The crowd started counting down as the giant lighted ball rose beside the stage. "Ten. Nine. Eight…" they chanted, quickly getting to "Three. Two. One!"

The Sons of Nashville launched into a country-twang version of "Auld Lang Syne." She had the vague notion that Deke was supposed to be leading the singing but he was too busy kissing her and that was all right by her.

"Happy New Year," he murmured against her lips.

Yes. It truly was. "I love you."

And that's when fireworks lit up the sky—and her heart.

Epilogue

Quin faced the mirror, shocked at the reflection of the woman staring back at her. In the background, the Bee Dubyas buzzed like their namesake insect. The Barron Wives and her soon-to-be mother-in-law were…they were a force of nature. There was no other description. In just a few minutes, she would enter the ballroom at the Barron Hotel and say her vows, then she and Deke would formally adopt Noelle.

Katherine stepped up behind her. Before Quin could turn, the older woman draped a familiar pearl necklace around her neck and fastened the clasp. Pressing her cheek against Quin's, she whispered, "Welcome to the family, sweetie. Thank you for making my son so happy."

Quin had to blink hard to keep tears at bay as she reached up to touch the pearls. "They're beautiful."

"So are you, Quincy. So are you. When the time comes, I hope you'll share them with other Tate brides when my boys finally find their forevers."

"Of course I will!"

Smiling, Katherine turned her. "And then the necklace will come back to you and Deacon will place it around the throat of y'all's little girl when she goes to meet her own true love at the altar."

Ten minutes later, Quin joined the love of her life and the baby soon to be theirs, legally in addition to emotionally, in front of a bent willow arbor. Laced with peonies and lilies and Oklahoma blue ribbon, the arch was the perfect backdrop for their nuptials. Hunter, Deacon's oldest brother, stood as his best man. When the Bee Dubyas discovered she had no close female friends, they drew straws to see who would be her matron of honor. Quin thought it fitting when Cassidy, the first Barron bride, won.

Judge Nelligan read the rites, and Quin said, "I do" to the rest of her life.

"Are you trying to take advantage of me?" Quin's words were slightly slurred. Deke had finally managed their escape from the party downstairs and retreated to their suite. He'd gotten them both naked and in bed and now his tough trooper was being too cute for words.

His lips curved against her cheek. "Of course I am."

"Oh. Okay. Just checking." She giggled and hiccupped. "I knew that last glass of champagne was a mistake. I should have had cake instead."

He settled beside her, propped on one elbow. "The cake was awesome. Want me to go get you some?"

Quin laughed and his insides did that funny tightening, like a balloon expanding in his chest.

"You traipsing around naked might just break some poor woman's brain."

That made him laugh as he lowered his head to kiss her. After the kiss, he smoothed out her hair and just looked at her. He'd never thought he could love another so much. Yet here he was on his wedding night, in love with this woman. And their daughter. Their *daughter*. Noelle Katherine Tate.

She ran her fingers over his lips. "Why the big smile?"

Deke hadn't realized he'd been smiling, but the answer was easy. "Just happy, darlin'. And thinkin' about how much I love my wife and child." He waggled his brows. "Want to try makin' a brother or sister for Noelle?"

She waggled hers in reply. "Think you're up to the task?"

"Oh, heck, yeah."

"You know what they say, right?"

"About what?"

"Pride. Because…" Quin brushed her fingertips down his bare chest and they dipped below the sheet. She curled her hand around him. "Just as I suspected. You are definitely full of pride."

He covered a groan with a deep chuckle. Quin knew *exactly* how to get his attention and he loved her touch. Deke leaned over and savored her skin as he nipped and licked his way down her neck. She tasted delicious and looked so sexy lying beneath him. He kissed her, deeply, not so much taking as sharing this time. As much as he wanted her, he wanted things slow and sweet tonight even as their bare flesh rubbed together, creating its own heat.

Breaking the kiss, he eased back. "Hello, wife."

Her smile wreathed her face. "Hello, husband."

"I do like the sound of that."

"Me, too."

The need for her zinged through Deke, like a new song, the words and melody teasing him until he was compelled to write them down. In this case, he was going to record them with his body on hers. In hers.

Quin shifted, her arms urging him back over her. She stretched, arched and pressed her lips against his heart. "This is mine," she murmured.

"Always," Deke promised. "Just like you'll always be mine."

He stroked his hand over her, arousing and teasing even as she continued to stroke him in the most intimate way. His eyes closed of their own accord as he absorbed the pleasure of what she did. He'd found where he belonged, found what he wanted in life.

"Are you ready, darlin'?"

Her eyes sparkled with desire as she opened her thighs for him. He shifted between them and gazed down at the woman who completed his life. "I never thought I'd ever say this, but damn if you aren't sexy in those pearls."

Her peal of laughter was cut short as he slid deep inside her. Here was comfort. Here was love. This country boy had finally come home.

Wrapped around each other, they made slow, sweet love that quickly turned hard and fast, their need and desire swamping them both. When Quin fell over the edge, Deke was there to catch her. The same way she held him through his own climax a few moments later. Panting, she rested her temple against his scruffy jaw.

"Wow," she sighed. "That was so much better than cake."

Deke laughed and Quin laughed with him. Life with his tough Christmas cop would never be a piece of cake. And he'd have it no other way.

* * * * *

Don't miss any of these cowgirl romances from Silver James.

COWGIRLS DON'T CRY
THE COWGIRL'S LITTLE SECRET
THE BOSS AND HIS COWGIRL
CONVENIENT COWGIRL BRIDE
REDEEMED BY THE COWGIRL

Available now from Harlequin Desire!

If you're on Twitter, tell us what you think of Harlequin Desire! #harlequindesire.

COMING NEXT MONTH FROM

HARLEQUIN *Desire*

Available November 7, 2017

#2551 THE TEXAN TAKES A WIFE
Texas Cattleman's Club: Blackmail • by Charlene Sands
Erin Sinclair's one-night stand with sexy cowboy Daniel Hunt is just what she needs. But when she offers to help out a friend and ends up working with someone *very* familiar, she'll soon learn just how determined a cowboy can be!

#2552 TWINS FOR THE BILLIONAIRE
Billionaires and Babies • by Sarah M. Anderson
Real estate mogul Eric Jenner is more than willing to work with his childhood friend Sofia. The single mom needs to provide for her adorable twins. But will combining business and pleasure lead to love...or to heartbreak?

#2553 LITTLE SECRETS: HOLIDAY BABY BOMBSHELL
by Karen Booth
Hotel heiress Charlotte Locke vows to best her commitmentphobic ex Michael Kelly in a business battle. But when he learns she's having his child, he'll have to convince her he'll do right by their child—and her heart—or risk losing her forever.

#2554 EXPECTING A LONE STAR HEIR
Texas Promises • by Sara Orwig
To fulfill a promise, US Army Ranger Mike Moretti goes home to Texas to work on the Warner ranch. His attraction to the owner—his friend's widow—is a temptation he can't resist, and then she announces a little surprise...

#2555 TWELVE NIGHTS OF TEMPTATION
Whiskey Bay Brides • by Barbara Dunlop
Mechanic Tasha Lowell is not his type. She's supposed to be repairing CEO Matt Emerson's yacht, not getting under his skin. But when a charity-ball makeover reveals the sensuous woman underneath the baggy clothes, Matt knows he must have her...

#2556 WRANGLING THE RICH RANCHER
Sons of Country • by Sheri WhiteFeather
When reclusive rancher Matt Clark, the troubled son of a famous country singer, confronts the spunky Libby Penn about her biography of his estranged father, anger and distrust might be replaced with something a whole lot more dangerous to his heart...

HDCNM1017

Get 2 Free Books,
Plus 2 Free Gifts—
just for trying the Reader Service!

HARLEQUIN *Desire*

SPECIAL EXCERPT FROM

HARLEQUIN® *Desire*

To fulfill a promise, US Army Ranger Mike Moretti goes home to Texas to work on the Warner ranch. His attraction to the owner—his friend's widow—is a temptation he can't resist, and then she announces a little surprise…

Read on for a sneak peek of
EXPECTING A LONE STAR HEIR
by USA TODAY *bestselling author Sara Orwig, the first book in her new* **TEXAS PROMISES** *series.*

As Mike stepped out of the car, his gaze ran over the sprawling gray stone mansion that looked as if it should be in an exclusive Dallas suburb instead of sitting on a mesquite-covered prairie.

After running his fingers through his wavy ebony hair, Mike put on his broad-brimmed black Stetson. As he strode to the front door, he realized he had felt less reluctance walking through minefields in Afghanistan. He crossed the wide porch that held steel-and-glass furniture with colorful cushions, pots of greenery and fresh flowers. He listened to the door chimes and in seconds, the ten-foot intricately carved wooden door swung open.

He faced an actual butler.

"I'm Mike Moretti. I have an appointment with Mrs. Warner."

"Ah, yes, we're expecting you. Come in. I'm Henry, sir. If you'll wait here, sir, I'll tell Mrs. Warner you've arrived."

"Thank you," Mike replied, nodding at the butler, who turned and disappeared into a room off the hall.

Henry reappeared. "If you'll come with me, sir, Mrs. Warner is in the study." Mike followed him until Henry stopped at an open door. "Mrs. Warner, this is Mike Moretti."

"Come in, Mr. Moretti," she said, smiling as she walked toward him.

He entered a room filled with floor-to-ceiling shelves of leather-bound books. After the first glance, he forgot his surroundings and focused solely on the woman approaching him.

Mike had seen his best friend Thane's pictures of his wife—one in his billfold, one he carried in his duffel bag. Mike knew from those pictures that she was pretty. But those pictures hadn't done her justice because in real life, Vivian Warner was a downright beauty. She had big blue eyes, shoulder-length blond hair, flawless peaches-and-cream complexion and full rosy lips. The bulky, conservative tan sweater and slacks she wore couldn't fully hide her womanly curves and long legs.

What had he gotten himself into? For a moment he was tempted to go back on his promise. But as always, he would remember those last hours with Thane, recall too easily Thane dying in a foreign land after fighting for his country, and Mike knew he had to keep his promise.

His only hope was that he wouldn't be spending too much time with Thane's widow.

Don't miss
EXPECTING A LONE STAR HEIR
by USA TODAY bestselling author Sara Orwig,
available November 2017 wherever
Harlequin® Desire books and ebooks are sold.

www.Harlequin.com

HDEXP1017

Want to give in to temptation with
steamy tales of irresistible desire?

Check out **Harlequin® Presents®**,
Harlequin® Desire and
Harlequin® Kimani™ Romance books!

New books available every month!

CONNECT WITH US AT:

Harlequin.com/Community

**ROMANCE WHEN
YOU NEED IT**

PGENRE2017

LOVE
Harlequin
romance?

Join our Harlequin community to share your thoughts and connect with other romance readers!

Be the first to find out about promotions, news, and exclusive content!

Sign up for the Harlequin e-newsletter and download a free book from any series at
www.TryHarlequin.com

CONNECT WITH US AT:

Harlequin.com/Community

 Facebook.com/HarlequinBooks

Twitter.com/HarlequinBooks

Instagram.com/HarlequinBooks

Pinterest.com/HarlequinBooks

ReaderService.com

 **HARLEQUIN®**

**ROMANCE WHEN
YOU NEED IT**

HSOCIAL2017